D1469306

TEN FINGERS TOUCHING

A tale of true love, mystery and adventure

Written by

Ellen A. Roth

Illustrated by

John Blumen

ISBN: 0990726827

ISBN 13: 9780990726821

Library of Congress Control Number: 2014916292

Published by Getting to the Point, Inc., Pittsburgh, PA

Printed in the United States of America * First Edition

This story is dedicated to the youth in every woman.

Contents

ACKNOWLEDGMENTS

More than a story, this book represents a dream come true. It brings to fruition a fairy tale that I began writing long ago. Throughout the evolution of *Ten Fingers Touching*, I enjoyed the support, advice and friendship of many wonderful people.

I am deeply grateful to my editor, Steve Fine, and my illustrator, John Blumen—two exceptionally gifted individuals whom I did not know at the beginning of this project.

Steve dedicated himself to editing the manuscript with skill and sensitivity. His thorough reviews of many drafts taught me to be a better writer. John's extraordinary talent and magnificent illustrations breathed life into the characters. Every time I look at the cover, I smile. I treasure not only Steve's and John's significant contributions but their friendships as well.

Special thanks go to celebrated mystery writer Jeffrey Siger for encouraging me to publish the story and to share it with others. I am also very grateful to Ramona DeFelice Long and Beverly Loy Taylor for their diligent, specialized editing pertaining to content and grammar, respectively. Other professionals who read the manuscript and offered helpful insights include Rachel Ekstrom and Kelly Rottmund.

My company, Getting to the Point, Inc., has a wonderful book club. Many thanks to the members who read the story and especially to those who provided detailed critiques including Kathy Azar, Mary Frances Cooper, Joanna Huss, Colleen Schabdach, Ann Zalla and, above all, Lida Larsen.

I am indebted to author Raymond Vennare for the introduction to Steve Fine and to author Nancy Martin for the introduction to Ramona DeFelice Long.

Finally, I appreciated the valuable comments from my children, Alexandra Kahn, Elizabeth Roth and Dr. Jonathan Roth. Most of all, I thank my husband, Dr. Loren Roth, for sharing with me the joy that true love brings to life.

Prologue

Ten toes overlapping
Ten fingertips pressing
Five senses blending
Two hearts merging
Minds converging
Each half-soul swirling
In the universe
Unites and pours into
One seamless skin,

A perfect whole.

Chapter One

Once Upon a Time in a Faraway Land

The malice that fed Evil simmered inside him as he impatiently gazed skyward. He had waited far too long for this meeting. In contrast, Good was in no rush to appear. She bided her time before bursting through the Heavens on a magnificent chariot drawn by four white, winged horses with long tails and flowing manes, leaving a dazzling display of white crystals in her wake. Draped in a white gown, Good was a handsome woman with natural beauty etched by years of wise governing and maturity.

Slithering out from the shadows, Evil quickly morphed from a small, spiky reptile into one of his infinite incarnations—a fierce, 50-foot-tall dragon that reared on two legs, breathing smoke and fire and roaring with wicked intent. Just as suddenly, the dragon twisted like a corkscrew, emitted a high-pitched whirring noise, and then spiraled downward into a new form—a thin, angular man in courtly dress that gave him a pleasing appearance, belying the evil glint in his eye.

Good burst through the Heavens on a magnificent chariot drawn by four white, winged horses with long tails and flowing manes, leaving a dazzling display of white crystals in her wake.

Good and Evil confronted one another at the confluence of the three rivers, where two mighty bodies of water joined together to form a third.

How did this fateful meeting come about, and where would it lead?

Evil had long been banished from the Kingdom by the forces of Good. After so many years in exile, his mounting rage had reached a crescendo, and he was more determined than ever to regain his presence and power. As he had done at least once each century for millennia, he petitioned for a meeting with Good, and she granted him a brief reprieve from his expulsion.

Standing face to face with Evil, Good eyed him with disdain.

"So wonderful to see you after all these years, my esteemed opponent," Evil began, accentuating his sarcasm with a deep, mocking bow.

Good was not amused. "State your purpose for requesting this meeting, so I may be done with you and on my way," she commanded.

Undaunted, the elegantly dressed man pressed on. "The people of this realm no longer deserve your protection," Evil asserted. "Your subjects are not as good or as virtuous as you would like to believe. They only restrain their impulses. If you have so much faith in the people under your influence, why do you still fear a test of their worthiness?"

Good had resisted this taunt for generations, but on this particular day she considered his thoughts before responding. "You are no wiser than when we last met many years ago," she replied. "The passing of time does not make your assumptions any truer, or your faults and ambitions less abhorrent. I will agree to a test this time, if only to show how wrong you are, so I may silence you and drive you away forever."

Barely able to contain his delight, Evil proposed what seemed to be the simplest of tests. "If virtue exists, then nothing can come between two virgin lovers' desire for one another on their wedding night," he declared. "Their passion will be all consuming and they will reach for each other above all else."

Evil held up a tarnished globe, its finish dull and unremarkable. "On the wedding night of two lovers you select for their unquestioned virtue, I shall place this globe before them. If they reach for it and take it into their hands before embracing one another, you will release me from your control and I will be free to roam the Kingdom once more."

Good never imagined that lovers of her choosing would find an inanimate object more desirable than each other's touch, let alone such an unattractive object, but she remained wary of Evil's deceitfulness. She agreed to his proposal but insisted on a caveat. "If the lovers fail the test, you do not win outright. Instead, I demand that the challenge you propose be passed along to their children, should their union produce offspring. Specifically, if a second child of their union passes its eighth birthday without either the firstborn or the second born touching the globe, you will be banished from the Kingdom forever."

The bargain made, Evil danced and twirled with delight. He knew that once the globe was placed before the young lovers, its tarnish would melt away under their gaze to reveal a golden, iridescent orb that glowed as intensely as their love. They would be unable to restrain their impulses and would reach for the globe before one another. Gleefully, he began to calculate how he would assert his dominance once he regained power.

As for any children that might come of this union, his loyal minions would eliminate them. With no children in the way, Evil would be free to grow in strength and overtake the Kingdom.

Good chose for the test her most precious subjects, two who embodied all that was virtuous and whose impending marriage was destined to change the world. They were Good's favorites, and their allegiance to and faith in her power were strong and unyielding.

Yet on their wedding night, Evil's trickery triumphed. When the young lovers approached their marriage bed, they found a tarnished globe nestled among the pillows. As they stared at the unexpected object, it quickly transformed into a magnificent, glowing, golden orb of great beauty. Unable to resist the lure of the object that shone as brightly as their love, they both reached out in wonder to touch it.

Every candle in the Kingdom flickered, and for a brief moment shadows veiled the land. Evil rejoiced at his dark success and the release of his long-restrained force.

Good watched helplessly the betrayal of the young lovers' innocence. As Evil's treacherous power surged anew, an unprecedented fury rose up inside Good. Her rage thundered and the earth trembled as she vowed to banish Evil forever.

The battle between Good and Evil had begun in earnest.

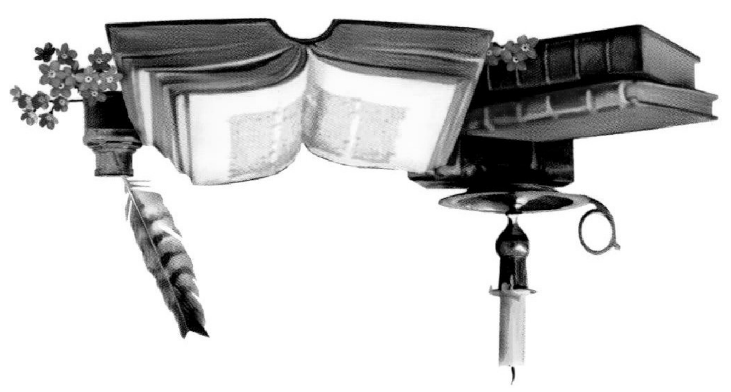

Chapter Two

THE MAIDEN AND THE PRINCESS

20 Years Later

Marianna sat quietly, slowly swirling her spoon in her morning tea. Peering into the teacup, she caught a distorted reflection of herself, so unlike the clarity with which she thought about the natural world. On this particular morning, she was absorbed in pondering the difference between twilight and dusk.

With long, honey-colored tresses and deep-blue eyes that flashed violet in moments of merriment, Marianna was a beautiful maiden. Her slender, graceful figure complemented her gentle ways and generous spirit, while a keen perceptiveness and interest in nature heightened her awareness of unusual changes in the world around her.

Marianna was only in her eighteenth year, but she sensed that storms were now stronger, dragons were now fiercer, and ominous, wavering shadows were appearing with ever-greater frequency in her village and the surrounding countryside. Sometimes, shadowy tentacles crossed the sun's path and obscured it for brief periods. Other times, shadows swept along the ground and then wrapped themselves around buildings. Marianna could not determine a logical explanation for her disconcerting observations. Life was so busy that neither she nor any of the other villagers fully grasped the significance of the changes or knew of Evil's growing dominion over the island Kingdom.

The only child of elderly parents, Marianna was born after they had long given up hope of ever being able to conceive. She was their gift from the Heavens, and she bathed their lives in the glow of her warmth and unfolding intelligence.

From the moment Marianna could focus her eyes, her father, a retired schoolteacher, taught her all he knew about the world. She learned to read and write, and studied mathematics, astronomy and music. She could identify the varieties of flora and fauna encountered in daily life, as well as decipher ancient texts. Although she had never traveled beyond the Kingdom, she could speak many tongues from distant lands whose geography, histories and customs she also knew well.

Marianna's mother was kind and warmhearted. She had served as midwife to the court and, on one occasion, to the Queen herself. She was well-respected for her loyalty to the royal family and for her discretion.

When word came to the palace that Marianna possessed prodigious intelligence, she was brought to the grand court to be the governess for the Princess.

Christened Rosalind Cordelia Theresa Miranda Victoria, the Princess was ordained Keeper of the Flame of Innocence.

While the King and Queen were tall and lean, the Princess, at the age of seven, had a fullness about her—a round little face with delightful dimples and a head full of curly, chestnut-brown hair that seemed incapable of being controlled. Her long locks cascaded down her back, while tiny wisps escaped from the decorative headbands that matched her dresses and framed her sweet face and smile. At the court and throughout the Kingdom, she was known as Princess Rosy, a name that both reflected and described her personality.

The Princess tried to attend to the beginnings of reading and writing, but she did not enjoy academic studies and her mind often wandered during Marianna's lessons. Rosy also lacked the patience to learn customary female pastimes like stitchery and weaving. What she loved was music and theatrics. Despite gentle reminders to modulate her voice, the child's melodic singing often echoed throughout the palace, heralding her appearance.

High-spirited and impish, Rosy was drawn to favorites like the notoriously funny court jester. She adored spending time with him and marveled at his ability to juggle, eat fire, throw bones, sing, dance and make people laugh.

While Marianna and the Princess enjoyed a close and loving relationship, it did not prevent Rosy from keeping a secret from her governess and everyone else at court—a secret she shared only with the jester. Rosy was very curious about other children and life beyond the palace walls. The jester, lacking in judgment and wanting to please the child, showed the Princess hidden passageways that allowed her to sneak from the castle unseen. From time to time, undetected by guards or servants, the Princess disguised herself in common clothing and escaped to seek out playmates in the village.

Her comedic personality made her very popular with most children, but the Princess was especially drawn to one very athletic boy. He and Rosy were the same age and each seemed to know the other's thoughts long before either said a word. They also argued a lot, which only seemed to make them closer. His name was Tanner, and he was one of three children born to Good's most favored couple.

So by day, Marianna tutored her mischievous but lovable student, and at dusk the maiden left the palace to return home and care for her parents. There was a rhythm to her days that kept her busy and she was grateful for the blessings in her life.

Chapter Three

THE MASTER OF THE FOREST

Raised in deep woods not far from Marianna's village, Martak never knew his parents. For as long as he could remember, he had lived with a mysterious adventurer. This Guide, Good's chosen warrior, treated Martak as a son and instructed him in woodlore and survival, as no boy had ever been schooled before. Martak was an attentive student and a quick learner. His Guide's training was augmented by lessons Martak gleaned from his daily encounters with animals of all kinds, for in this forest, woodland creatures coexisted with their jungle brethren. His days were occupied with endless hours of practice in tracking, hunting, archery and self-defense. At night he listened raptly for hours as his Guide spun stories filled with bold, courageous deeds and sage advice.

Martak loved the land and had great empathy for all wildlife. There was no forest creature, large or small, that he feared or misunderstood—and for some reason known only to the Heavens, they understood him as well and kept a watchful eye on him from the time of his infancy.

As a young child, Martak had been enthralled with birds and dreamed of flying. Toddlers are often attracted to shiny pebbles, but Martak was drawn to feathers from the first time he discovered one on the forest floor.

When he was five years old, he would stand on a boulder and jump into the air while wildly flapping his arms, only to tumble to the ground. The forest folk watched with amusement as the boy "cub" never tired of imitating one of their kind.

As the years went by, Martak amassed a vast collection of feathers. His Guide humored him by fashioning a set of wings with a wide span, glued together with tree sap and tied with sinew to a leather body harness. His Guide warned him not to be reckless with the wings, but Martak was fearless and determined to fly.

Unbeknownst to his Guide, Martak took his wings up to a cliff, strapped on his harness and took a leap of faith. He spiraled out of control toward the sea and his likely demise, when golden eagles flew to his rescue, swooping under him and straightening his flight path. The eagles showed him how to catch the wind and gracefully flap his broad wings so he could soar to great heights, turn on a tight angle, dive through the air and land safely.

From then on, Martak enjoyed his communion with the golden eagles. Their wings, he admired. Their talons, he respected. And their bravery, he shared. He practiced gliding with them daily, mastering their maneuvers and learning how to navigate the sky. In turn, his persistence, courage and success resonated with the mighty eagles. The boy and the majestic birds formed an unshakable bond.

Just as he flew with the grace of an eagle, Martak swam as if taught by a mother dolphin and moved with the agility of a jungle cat. Even his Guide was awed by the feats the boy achieved in the air, under water and on land.

Martak was happy growing up in the forest and never at a loss for companionship among the animals. He enjoyed wrestling with the young lions, playing fetch with the leopards and boxing with bear cubs, even when a solid bear-paw swing sent him sailing across the glen. But he was also curious about the world around him and life in the village.

From time to time, he would climb a tree or hide among the bushes to observe village youth his age doing their chores or playing games. It made him wonder about his own family and if they lived nearby, and why he had been raised apart from them.

Martak had no idea of the secret that brought him to his forest life. His Guide helped him to learn many things but always seemed reluctant to point Martak toward any understanding of his birth.

Young Martak grew to manhood, tall and strong. Fierce as the lion of his spirit, he had tawny locks to match. Yet behind his dark-green eyes nestled a gentle and compassionate soul who had earned the friendship and respect of the forest creatures. It might have surprised anyone who did not know him well that neither a mother's loving hand nor even a woman's touch were familiar to him.

But that was soon to change.

He heard the laughter and even before seeing her, he was in love.

Martak had been tracking a lost fawn to lead it back to the herd. His skill had brought him within a few yards of fulfilling his mission when he discovered far more. His trained body remained motionless and his gaze never faltered, but his heart beat like the wings of a hummingbird as he gazed upon the most beautiful maiden he had ever seen. With flowers in her hair and clover in her hands, the maiden fed the quivering fawn while an older woman searched the sky, observing that the day was passing far too quickly.

"Marianna, let's go back to the village before your father comes looking for us," the older woman admonished. "You know how he worries when we are not home before dusk."

"All right, Mother, but what about this fawn?" Marianna replied. "He's all alone. Maybe we should take him with us?"

Smiling, Marianna's mother stroked her daughter's hair. "No, my dear, you know that forest creatures must roam free. He'll find his way!" Hesitantly, Marianna started toward the path home and away from Martak's breathless stare. Suddenly, the air currents shifted and the fawn bolted. Marianna and her mother quickly turned in the direction of windswept leaves and saw a man standing still as a monument.

Even fully clothed, Martak would have startled them. But wearing little more than what he was tracking, his appearance froze the women in place. They were unable to avert their gaze, yet strangely not alarmed. All seemed steeped in some calming ether. To Marianna, he looked more regal a personage than anyone she had ever seen in her young Princess's court.

"We must go now, Marianna." Her mother broke the silence with uncharacteristic firmness. The words sounded to Marianna as if born of something unstated and not just concern about the sun's lingering rays. A mysterious reaction, she thought, as she reluctantly turned to leave the glen and the stranger.

That night, as Marianna lay in her bed, she knew where the following day would take her.

Chapter Four

EXPLORING THE OUTDOORS

Marianna awoke, hardly having slept at all. Rushing to her bedroom window, she flung open the shutters to reveal a magnificent dawn. There had been a severe storm during the night, but now the sun rose, bright and warm. The sky was cloudless, the air scrubbed fresh by the rains, and every garden in sight had seemingly bloomed overnight. The world never looked greener or lusher. On such a glorious day, it occurred to her that the ominous shadows she occasionally noticed were not real, but simply reflections of her overthinking.

When she reached her young charge, Marianna was flushed with excitement. She had already arranged with the cook for a picnic lunch when she greeted Rosy in the classroom.

"Good morning, my Princess," Marianna announced with enthusiasm. "This is such a beautiful day that we are going outside for our lessons. I will teach you about plants and animals in their natural environments."

"Oh, yes, yes!" exclaimed the Princess, her dimples deepening in a big smile. Jumping up and down and clapping her hands with innocent delight, she bounded toward the palace gates, not wasting an instant lest her teacher change her mind.

The maiden and the Princess explored nature, wandering in the direction of the glen where Marianna had seen the mysterious stranger.

Marianna followed more gracefully, extending greetings to staff and guards as she exited the palace. Together, the maiden and the Princess set out hand in hand to explore nature, singing songs and wandering in the direction of the glen where Marianna had seen the mysterious stranger. They stopped frequently along the way to study wildflowers, observe animals and listen to the symphony of outdoor sounds. Both teacher and student made daisy chains for their hair and collected wonderfully shaped leaves, interesting rocks and fresh berries. By the time they reached the clearing where Marianna had seen the mysterious stranger, they both were famished.

While Princess Rosy rummaged through their picnic basket in search of palace treats, Marianna looked around, carefully observing how the sun's rays illuminated the lush greenery and clusters of brightly flowering plants erupting between the boulders. Nothing seemed out of the ordinary, causing her to wonder if she had really seen a man, nearly naked, yet totally at one with himself and the environment. Or had she just imagined him? There was no trace of his presence.

She could not see him, but he was there.

Chapter Five

SHADOWS IN THE GLEN

After the maiden and her mother left the glen, Martak could not tear himself away from the place where Marianna had stood. He remained there entranced, his mind and heart focused on only one thing—finding and absorbing whatever sense of her still lingered.

Dusk began to cloak the forest and Martak still had not stirred until an unfamiliar sound jolted his attention, and he realized he was not alone. He perceived the flickering presence of a nearby figure, but not one of his familiar forest creatures. The elusive figure moved quickly, casting a shadow to conceal its presence in the growing darkness.

Martak grew increasingly angry with himself. *Who is this shadow maker, what is its purpose and how long has it been here?* He had been so immersed in thoughts of the maiden that he forgot his Guide's cardinal rule—be forever alert to your surroundings. Now he was at risk.

It was then that he heard the *thhhk* of the arrow leaving its bowstring and he fell to the ground with the swiftness of a flame doused by water, but far from extinguished, as his instincts saved him. Unhurt, Martak rolled to his left and came up with his own bow drawn. Hurling an arrow in the direction of the would-be assassin, he simultaneously darted from the clearing and toward the protection of the forest. Running for safety, he wondered who had fired at him and why? The bowman was not the shadow maker, because the arrow came from the opposite side of the glen. Martak had no enemies he was aware of and carried no valuables upon him to rob. He repeated the questions over and over again in his mind: *Who is after me? Why am I a target? Why did the attacker stop after one try?*

Perhaps clues remained on the other side of the glen. Without hesitating, Martak left the refuge of the dense trees and slowly, silently, crept to where his arrow had landed.

By now it was quite late. Clouds were beginning to obscure the moon and the wind was mounting. As Martak approached the spot where his arrow had fallen, he heard a whirring noise, much like he had heard once when a frightened deer, fleeing across a stream, was drawn into a whirlpool. Cautiously and with a fresh arrow readied, he moved stealthily toward the mysterious sound.

Peering from behind a large boulder, Martak saw little but a broken bow and his arrow nearby. Suddenly, a burst of lightning, a precursor of the coming storm, split the air and lit the ground, allowing a fuller glimpse of the scene. There was a circular mound of earth that formed a ring around a hole, but before he could explore it with his hands, the

Heavens that had gifted him with a sliver of light erased what had been revealed. A violent storm erupted, washing away every trace of the events that had just occurred.

Martak longed to find his Guide and tell him about the maiden and the perilous attack, but first he had to seek shelter from the storm bearing down on him. He turned from the glen and moved quickly to a nearby cave, where he lay down on a bed of leaves to sleep. But his mind refused to rest, focusing instead on the day's events as he tossed and turned.

Eventually succumbing to exhaustion, Martak fell into a deep sleep. His dreams drew him away from the dangers of the evening to visions of the maiden and matters of his heart.

Dreams were nothing new to Martak. He looked forward to them, for in them he often found direction. In this dream, he saw a light bathing the maiden in the glen, a light that never dimmed, and he knew she was his destiny.

He also dreamed of a cherubic girl, laughing and giggling alongside the maiden—and a boy who trailed them. The boy walked with a bit of a swagger and a lot of bravado, and he was preoccupied with kicking small stones long distances. Martak could not quite understand this dream, but it did not bother him because he knew there was still much to learn.

Chapter Six

Observations

As fiercely as the storm shrouded the night in pelting rain, dawn emerged with a gentle counterpoint of sunshine and cloudless skies. Just as Marianna had awakened fresh with excitement, Martak arose to a glorious new day, even as he recalled the sinister events of the preceding evening.

Martak slipped out of the cave and onto a rocky cliff overlooking a deep lake. His perfect muscles glistened in the morning light as he leaped into a magnificent swan dive, carrying him to the water so gracefully that his entry caused barely a ripple. Burdened by recollections of the night's troubling events, a lesser athlete might have flawed his performance. But Martak's unparalleled physical skills were innate and unerring, like a bird's ability to fly or a tiger's lethal pounce.

He emerged from the water and discovered a patch of wild strawberries. He plucked the fruit and ate slowly, while his mind raced to sort through all that had happened in such a short time.

As a young boy, Martak had learned that the best place to think and gain perspective was from the heights of a tree. He spied a stately oak and with the suppleness of a jaguar made his way to a secure branch near the top.

From this vantage point, he could see for miles, and before noon, he caught sight of two charming figures approaching the glen. His heart beat faster when he recognized the maiden who now filled his thoughts and being with passion, and a young companion who, coincidentally, resembled the playful little girl from his dreams. His visions had indeed foretold the future.

Martak could not take his eyes off Marianna as she drew near. His heart ached with the desire to be close to her. Yet he feared that if he suddenly appeared, she might flee and he wanted to savor her presence for as long as he could. He knew from the way she wistfully looked around that, like him, she had been drawn back to the spot where they had previously met, and it confirmed to him that their destinies were linked. The thought filled him with awe and pleasure, and he smiled with true joy.

Perched among the treetops, Martak watched Marianna and Princess Rosy for much of the day until, overcome by yearning and curiosity, he could no longer stay so far away. He descended and edged closer to the pair without snapping so much as a twig. Hidden from view, he could overhear their conversation and Marianna's earnest tone.

"My Princess, it's getting late," Marianna entreated. "We need to head back to the palace."

"Oh, no. I don't want to go," implored the child. "This has been the best day of my life. Couldn't we stay just a little longer?"

"Rosy, we can come back another day, but now we really should be on our way so we'll be home in time for tea."

"Marianna, pleeease, pleeease. Let's just play one game of hide-and-seek before we have to leave. You know it's my favorite."

Against her better judgment, Marianna curtsied deeply as if to the Queen and in a humorously mocking voice replied, "Yes, Your Majesty, a quick game of hide-and-seek."

As Marianna covered her eyes and slowly counted, Princess Rosy scampered into the woods. Their rule was at the count of twenty, you had to stop wherever you were and hide. But the Princess, delightfully overwhelmed by freedom, ignored the rule this time, forgot her boundaries and continued to run deeper into the forest, unaware of any danger that might be present.

Reaching twenty, Marianna opened her eyes and began looking in all directions for the Princess. She searched behind the ancient trees, under thick vegetation, among the flowering bushes and around giant boulders. Unable to find the child, Marianna first called, and then screamed, "Rosy!" With no response, her fear escalated rapidly, engulfing her in a sea of panic. *Where could the Princess be? How could I have let this happen?*

Marianna was filled with guilt and terror as she searched and called Rosy's name. She knew that fierce, wild animals roamed the forest and dragons stalked the region. Every horrible thing that could befall Rosy rushed to Marianna's mind. Running through the thicket, screaming Rosy's name, Marianna's neatly pinned hair tore loose and whipped about her shoulders. Eyes wide with fright, she hardly noticed her gown ripping as it caught in the briars. Never had an insane woman looked more crazed than Marianna at this lowest moment in her life.

Martak witnessed it all and knew what he had to do.

Chapter Seven

Danger

Until now, Martak had never observed maternal love among his own kind. But he had grown up watching the protective instincts of animals that give birth in the wild, and as a young lad he had once intruded upon a she-bear preening her cubs. The memories, along with the scars from that episode, helped him understand what he was now witnessing.

The little girl was racing about with the careless abandon of innocent youth, confident that maternal watchfulness cloaked her with invulnerability. But the maiden knew better and it showed. Martak's heart felt Marianna's pain and fear. He longed to comfort her and lead her to the Princess. But remembering the she-bear, he still believed that to appear suddenly before her in the woods would not be wise. Instead, he moved to protect the Princess while guiding Marianna to her.

Martak glided through the forest toward the sound of the Princess's footsteps and voice. It was easy for him to locate her. In fact, it would not have been a challenge for any hunter to follow her. After all, a seven-year-old child skipping through the woods and singing over and over again, "I'm a princess you can't find, ha-ha, ha-ha," does not take extraordinary tracking talent.

When Martak found Rosy, he saw that others had discovered her as well. Ignorant of the menacing eyes watching and the jaws ready to devour her, Rosy sat quietly next to a stream, tossing pebbles into the water and wondering when Marianna would appear.

Ignorant of the menacing eyes watching and the jaws ready to devour her, Rosy sat quietly next to a stream, tossing pebbles into the water.

But Martak knew well the danger Rosy faced. The predators stalking her were merciless, for they had their own young to feed. It was life and death for them and he understood that was how it had to be. Still, it was not a lesson he thought the Princess needed to experience. Nor did he want to alert her to threats that might forever change her innocent view of life.

Instead, and ever so softly, Martak began to whistle. It was the gentle tone of a songbird—but one the watching predators knew did not inhabit their woods. They pricked their ears as the notes deepened and then suddenly burst into the golden eagle's piercing cry. And then they all knew that the child by the stream was under Martak's protection and thus under theirs, for Martak was the Master of the Forest—not by reason of his birth, but by reason of his deeds.

Rosy also heard the bird and when it exploded into the cry of the eagle, she dropped her pebbles and turned to search for the source of the fierce call. Strangely not frightened by the sound, the child found comfort in the unseen presence of its maker.

Marianna heard the piercing sound, too, but in her state of panic could not discern between good or evil. She just raced frantically in the direction of the intense cry, her mind fighting a host of horrible scenarios as she ran. Tripping over decayed trees, sliding down hillsides and fighting through brambles, she desperately struggled through the dense forest. Tattered, badly bruised and scraped, she burst upon the stream and Rosy.

Crazed yet blessedly relieved, Marianna rushed to the Princess, swooping her up and hugging her breathless. The tears streaming down Marianna's face startled Rosy more than her governess's outpouring words of love, scolding, self-recrimination and intense relief amid ever-tighter embraces.

Rosy, now also nearly in tears, continued to deny any wrongdoing, stammering innocently, "Why are you so angry with *me?* I've been waiting here for *you.*" Then, with the uninhibited objectivity of youth, she pointed at her governess and said, "You're bleeding."

Grasping each of Rosy's hands in her own and looking directly into her innocent eyes, Marianna exclaimed, "My Princess, you have frightened me more than I have ever been before. You don't know the dangers that could have befallen you, wandering so far into the forest. It's my fault and I am to blame. We should have gone home. I will never, ever take you beyond the castle gates again until you learn and fully understand how careful you must be."

"But, but—"

"Rosy, please! We'll talk about this later, but right now we must return to the palace," Marianna insisted. "It is getting late. We are lost. We have no food or shelter." As her fear escalated, Marianna's spirits fell even further. She had no idea how to get back and, in her mounting panic, she was alarming the child. She had to regain control of herself.

Leaning into the clear stream to scoop up a drink of cool water for the Princess, Marianna caught her reflection and, for the first time, she saw the torn gown, the cuts and bruises and how dreadful she looked. Her despair deepened, and it was about to get worse.

Rising to offer the water cupped in her hands to the Princess, Marianna suddenly sensed that the forest was unnaturally quiet. Tension hung in the still air. It was then that she saw them—the shapes of wild animals just beyond the tree line that encircled her and the Princess, the beasts' eyes staring intently from all directions. Despite her pounding heart and tightening throat, Marianna reacted quickly. She grabbed a thick, fallen branch from the forest floor and backed up to shield Rosy.

Marianna had never harmed a creature, but now her first instinct was to kill any aggressor that threatened their safety and defend the child with her own life. "Don't move, my Princess," Marianna warned. "Pretend you're a statue."

"Go away! Leave us alone!" Marianna shrieked, while vigorously swinging the branch in the air, prepared to bludgeon any animal that ventured within range of the club she wielded. Fear gave way as anger rose within her.

Her back pressed against Marianna, Rosy was stunned by her teacher's fierceness and wisely obeyed, scrunching her eyes tightly shut and freezing in place. But the child could not keep her eyes closed for long, and, when she opened them, she noticed a solitary figure standing at the edge of the trees.

"Don't worry, Marianna," Rosy said with remarkable calmness. "He'll help us."

Now it was Marianna's turn to be startled as she turned to see who Rosy was talking about and saw him standing at a respectful distance—the man she had hoped to see again.

Chapter Eight

THE MAGIC OF THE TOUCH

Martak observed the reunion of maiden and child with curiosity. He had never seen such an outburst of emotion and now that his mission had been accomplished, he was relieved to remain a short distance away. He made a mental note to ask his Guide to enlighten him about the female temperament, not realizing that it was always meant to be a mystery.

Emotionally drained, physically exhausted, filled with joy and pain, Marianna managed to give Martak a weak but grateful smile of appreciation. She started to take a step in his direction and then collapsed. In seconds, he was by her side. Gently scooping her listless body from the ground, he held her close to his chest. She felt weightless in his powerful arms. It was a defining moment for Martak. Holding her, he was enveloped by a sense of oneness and completeness that few ever experience. He felt more than he understood that this beautiful woman was his other half. He vowed to love and protect her for eternity.

Together, the young Princess and the Master of the Forest, carrying his beloved, walked out of the woods and toward the palace. When they reached the outskirts of the castle, Martak was uncharacteristically unsure how to proceed. This time, it was Princess Rosy's turn to come to the rescue.

Tugging at Martak's arm, she flashed a disarming smile and gleefully exclaimed, "Follow me!" Humming and skipping, she led him to a hidden tunnel that passed under the moat. "Princess, where does this passageway lead?" Martak asked with genuine surprise.

Suddenly realizing that she was about to expose her and the jester's secret, Rosy avoided Martak's gaze by looking down at her shoes, which were covered with dust from the day's adventures. "Inside. It goes inside," she mumbled, pointing in the direction of the castle.

"Can you get back by yourself?" Martak asked.

Nodding affirmatively, Rosy darted into the tunnel to avoid any further conversation that might get her deeper into trouble.

Having seen her disappearing act earlier in the day, Martak was not entirely confident of the Princess's sense of direction, so he summoned a battalion of fireflies to light the narrow passageway for her. Rosy ran through the tunnel and in no time was back in her royal bedroom as if it had been the most normal of days.

Marianna remained faint, and Martak enjoyed the intimacy of holding her against his chest and listening to her breathe. He knew it would be best to carry her to her home, but where did she live? Somewhere in the nearby village, he surmised, and headed that way. Turning in the direction of the thatched houses, he came to a little brook.

Martak set Marianna down on a soft bed of moss by the rivulet and began to gently cleanse her cuts and bruises. She awoke to the water's coolness, trying to assess where she was and remember what had happened. Her first thought was of Rosy, and Martak assured her that the child was safe in the palace. She thanked him with grateful words, but the look in her eyes expressed far more.

As he placed his hands upon her wounds, Marianna instinctively pressed her body deeper into the cool moss. Her eyes drew him toward her in a manner that her mind screamed was insane. She had not spoken to this stranger more than a moment, and yet she let him touch her as freely as she would touch herself. But this was not her mind leading the way. It was something else. Something she knew she would find only with him.

Martak made soft compresses of grasses and herbs to heal her injuries. He felt her body tense when he first placed his hands upon her. Yet as he gently touched her thigh with the soothing mixture, he felt the taut muscle relax in his hands. Slowly and tenderly, he stroked the bruises on her thigh, calf and ankle. When he reached her toes, he had no idea what to do next. As relaxed as her body had become, his was now as tight as a fully drawn bow. He dared not look in her eyes for guidance, for fear he could not control his passion.

At that moment, he first felt and then heard Marianna's soft, warm breath as it passed between her lips in a long, slow exhale. His eyes were uncontrollably drawn to hers and the burning violet intensity he found there. Overwhelmed by desire for one another, they both knew there could be no stopping.

Chapter Nine

The Poem

From the moment their love merged by the brook, the two were inseparable. Martak waited every day at the palace gates with his dappled gray mare for Marianna to finish work and he accompanied her home. Sometimes he held the reins of the high-spirited horse while he and Marianna walked hand in hand. Other times, he led her on horseback. The lovers always lingered, finding an excuse to delay their inevitable separation.

They instinctively understood one another, yet each reveled in the daily discoveries of what made the other so uniquely special.

He was the Master of the Forest and she was the Mistress of Books. What she gleaned from reading, he instinctively absorbed from the world around him.

She was as delicate and feminine as he was rugged and masculine.

Steady and centered, his physical prowess assured self-confidence. Although incredibly charming, she had a tendency to worry and obsess about things both real and imagined.

She loved to talk and he loved to listen. The music in her voice and the graceful gesturing of her hands as she spoke resonated in his heart. And yet when he spoke, his simple words penetrated to the core of the matter more eloquently than her refined vocabulary.

Yin to the other's yang, theirs was a union of opposites. His strengths complemented her weaknesses and what he lacked, she provided in abundance. Together they made a perfect whole. That these two souls were meant for one another had been heralded by the Heavens long ago.

Ten toes overlapping
Ten fingertips pressing

One afternoon, Martak and Marianna strolled near a pond. The place had special meaning for Martak and he wanted to share it with her. The day was magnificent and as they approached the water, Martak spontaneously swept Marianna off her feet and carried her to the pond's edge. He loved to hold her, to feel the softness of her skin and smell the fragrance of her hair. As always, she looked at him with those inviting eyes and his heart swelled with desire.

Five senses blending
Two hearts merging
Minds converging

He set her down on the ledge of the ancient stone wall surrounding the pond, then leaped into the water to pluck a lily from one of the myriad pads and presented it to her. Marianna removed the combs from her honey-colored hair, allowing it to cascade over her shoulders. The sun's rays bouncing off the glistening pond highlighted the golden wisps and created a glowing halo above her. With water lily in hand, she made an enchanting sight.

Dangling her feet in the pond, Marianna playfully splashed water at Martak. After several minutes of dodging drops, he suggested that she stop, lest she find herself among the frogs. Never one to back down from a challenge, Marianna kicked even more water in Martak's direction. Before she could escape, and true to his word, he grabbed her by the waist and effortlessly pulled her into the pond with him. As she looked up at him, protesting with feigned indignation, he kissed her forehead and then the tip of her nose. She arched her head backward and they found each other's lips as her arms wrapped around his neck.

Her gown was not meant for swimming and Marianna managed to unlace and slip out of it. Their nakedness was pure, innocent and free from shame. The water creatures rejoiced that their master had found a mate, and when the two lovers climbed out of the pond and rested on the grassy bank, the animals nearby ducked quietly and respectfully from sight.

Martak reached out to catch a trickle of water that started on Marianna's forehead and ran down the side of her face to her chin. Like a flower turns to the sun as its petals unfold, she leaned her cheek into his hand, and with her own hand pulled him toward her.

Each half soul swirling
In the universe
Unites and pours into
One seamless skin...

Her violet eyes gave him permission for what they both wanted. He explored with his hands and all of his senses the fullness of her being. With the sensitivity of a keen hunter and the gentleness of a gifted lover, Martak found the hills and valleys, crevices, foliage and hidden waters of her curvaceous terrain. Reveling in passion, he drove her to call his name.

Chapter Ten

THE REQUEST

"M*artak, Martak.*"

The words rang in his ears, but this time it was not Marianna's voice and he was not by the pond. He awoke in his own bed in the dwelling where he lived with his Guide. The shouting persisted, jolting him out of deep sleep and into reality.

"The King commands you to come to the palace at once!" the messenger hollered through the bolted door.

Martak leaped to his feet. "What for? Is Marianna hurt? Is the Princess all right?"

"Just come," was the hurried reply. "We must make haste."

Martak let out a high-pitched whistle and within seconds his mare appeared. Together, the Master of the Forest riding bareback and the messenger in his courtly attire galloped back to the castle.

Martak entered the great hall for the first time, and while he had never seen such splendor, he did not pause. Rushing past the ornately carved oak tables and magnificent wall tapestries, he dashed into the throne room and slid into a kneeling position. The King, also in motion, paced back and forth as he fought to collect his thoughts and the two men nearly collided. From the way the King tugged at his beard and pursed his lips, his distress and preoccupation were obvious.

The King drew Martak's gaze to the map and pointed with his scepter.

Sidestepping Martak's unceremonious entrance, the King commanded, "Rise, young man. I have heard much about you," and while carefully assessing Martak's demeanor, he added, "and I have much to tell you in confidence."

Martak had only seen the King from a distance when he addressed the villagers from the palace balcony on state occasions. As the King spoke, Martak was astonished to learn that the man standing before him with commanding posture and penetrating eyes was one battle away from losing his Kingdom to the forces of Evil.

Unfurling a large map of the island, the King showed Martak where the sea was becoming fiercer and violent storms were devastating coastal villages, flooding homes, destroying crops and drowning livestock. Mighty dragons were pounding the earth while monstrous, evil shadows, once confined to the northern provinces, now lurked along the coastline and were swooping inland.

"I have noticed strange sightings with greater frequency," the King emphasized. "Occasionally, unusual shadows cross the sun. Sometimes shadows slither over the earth and, upon returning from a recent hunt, I noticed shadows lingering on the palace walls. I am deeply disturbed by what I have seen. I believe Evil is behind these unnatural occurrences, and they are signs that his presence is growing nearer and stronger."

Speaking slowly and deliberately, the King continued. "Princess Rosy, Keeper of the Flame of Innocence, may be in great danger, for she is the key to halting the spread of evil and preserving good. Because of circumstances surrounding her birth, which I cannot disclose to you, the Princess must be protected from a curse that threatened our Kingdom long before she was born. The threat exists until she reaches her eighth birthday, now only a few days away." The King went on to explain and emphasized Rosy's unknowing role in the struggle that would determine the Kingdom's fate.

Watching Martak's reaction carefully, the King added, "I have taken measures to keep the Princess and the palace safe. Twice as many soldiers have been posted at the watchtowers and along every parapet, and guards have been stationed at every doorway within the palace.

"We must root out and destroy the source of evil before it has a chance to approach my daughter and tempt her with a golden, iridescent globe. For if she embraces it freely like the other innocents before her, there will be no stopping Evil's dominion.

"Martak, I know little of your past, but I am aware of your reputation as the Master of the Forest and a loyal subject," the King went on. "I have heard stories of your strength and bravery from the Princess, and Marianna assures me they are true."

The King drew Martak's gaze to the map and pointed with his scepter. "My scouts tell me that Evil lurks in the coves and inlets off our coastline," he continued. "I am asking you to captain a ship and lead a secret expedition to destroy Evil. Only then will the Princess and our Kingdom be truly safe. I know I can trust you to do this before any harm comes to her."

Martak had been ill at ease from the time he entered the palace, but this revelation from the King overwhelmed him. "Your Majesty, I would gladly give my life to protect the Princess, but I only know the ways of the forest," he struggled to reply. "I have never been at sea and I have no expertise in commanding a ship. I humbly beg your pardon but my abilities have been overestimated. There must be a better man to serve you on this mission."

"Not a better man," the King replied. "Perhaps one with more experience, but not one whom I could trust more than you. Think about what I have said, and come back in the morning with your final decision. We have little time to waste."

Chapter Eleven

Danger Persists

Martak left the palace enveloped in uncertainty. His horse was waiting for him, and he walked alongside the mare as he revisited his conversation with the King. His mind felt as if it had been bludgeoned by a blunt ax. Torn between duty and doubt, he stumbled along, trying to make sense of the King's daunting request.

Over and over he pondered. *This is my King and this is my country. I want to protect the Princess, not only for her own sake and that of the Kingdom, but also because of what she means to Marianna. But how can I captain a ship when I have never been at sea? How can I be responsible for the fate of a crew? For the fate of the Kingdom?*

Martak instinctively headed toward the forest and his Guide, hoping he would have answers to these desperately important questions. It was late in the day when he reached the edge of the woods. Still completely absorbed in his thoughts, he was no closer to a decision.

Out of nowhere, a lioness leaped in front of him. Martak never heard the arrow that pierced her belly, an arrow intended for his heart. As she crashed to the ground, a nearby shadow disappeared. Kneeling over the wounded animal, he heard a faint, now-familiar whirring sound from across the meadow. He fired an arrow in the direction of the strange noise, and should have run to save himself from the assassin, but he could not leave the injured lioness that had protected him. He gently pulled the arrow from her shuddering body. The gushing wound was mortal, and all he could do was hold her as life drained from her body.

Marianna waited at the drawbridge for Martak to walk her home, as was their custom. When he did not appear, her mind conjured the worst of scenarios, and it was then that she saw his mare charging in her direction. The horse knelt, coaxing Marianna onto its back, and once she wrapped her arms around its neck, the mare took off as if galloping into battle. Marianna hung on with all her strength, slipping and sliding across the horse's bare back, worrying desperately about what harm might have come to Martak and where she was being taken.

Marianna found Martak near the forest, drenched in blood and cradling the once-proud lioness in his arms. Forest creatures large and small surrounded him in a ring of mourners. She rushed to Martak's side and he looked up at her, the sorrow in his eyes meeting the horror in her own.

"Martak, my beloved, what happened? Are you all right?"

Martak quickly regained his composure and jumped to his feet, his animal instincts now on high alert. "Marianna, you must go home at once," he insisted. "It isn't safe for you here."

"No. No. No." She was adamant, hammering her fists together to underscore the intensity of her decision. "I can't leave you. I won't leave you. You must tell me what happened."

Martak shook his head. This was not the time for a lovers' quarrel or negotiations. He was willing to put his own life at risk, but there was no compromising Marianna's safety.

He spoke quietly but with authority. "I have many things to tell you. Many things I want to share with you. But first, there is something I need to do. Trust me and go home. I will come to you tonight and tell you everything." With that, he let out an eagle's cry and the forest creatures surrounded Marianna, forming a protective shield. With gentle persistence, they nudged her back toward the village as her mind spun with apprehension and a thousand questions.

Martak resumed his hunter's mentality and turned in the direction of the assassin, wondering how much worse the day could get. First, there was the King's daunting request, then a second attempt on his life and now Marianna showing up in the face of danger.

He pondered his two narrow escapes from death. *Were these incidents random or related? What did they have in common?* How could he explain everything to Marianna and would he ever reach his Guide? There was much to sort through and very little time.

Martak tried to make sense of the two assassination attempts. Both had caught him off guard when he was lost in thought following a momentous occasion—one heart-throbbing, one gut-wrenching. Both times, a shadow appeared in the opposite direction from where the bowman had fired at him, and in both cases, after the failed attempt, there was that whirring sound he could not place.

Now Martak crept once again in the direction of the strange sound. As he suspected, he found his arrow and a broken bow near a fresh mound of loose earth surrounding a circular hole, clearly not dug with claws or a snout.

The King was concerned about mysterious shadows that appeared unexpectedly, and Martak's experience with illusive, shadowy figures led him to surmise that the maker of the shadows was an agent of Evil. This Shadowmaker had just mercilessly eliminated another bowman for failing to succeed. The evidence suggested that both assassins had vanished by being sucked into the ground, as if into whirlpools of earth. Suffocation by live burial was each bowman's punishment for failure.

But the question lingered—why was Evil trying to kill him? Time was passing quickly, and soon he would need to give his answer to the King. Martak's head sought the advice of his Guide. But his heart pointed him elsewhere, and he turned his footsteps in the direction of the village.

Chapter Twelve

THE DECISION

Martak reached Marianna's house just as the moon appeared in the sky. His head ached with what he wanted to tell her, and her heart pulsed with questions she wanted to ask him. But all words were forgotten at first glance, as each found refuge in the other's arms. Martak embraced Marianna so tightly it seemed as if they shared one breath. They clung to each other, sensing that the day's events had changed their lives forever.

Hand in hand, Marianna led Martak to the fireplace. Seated on cushions before the flames, his eyes devoured her beauty as he sought to control his rising ardor. Her honey-colored hair flowed over her shoulders, glowing in the firelight and gifting her with a heavenly radiance.

Mesmerized, Martak reached over to take a wisp of hair that had fallen in Marianna's face and tenderly tucked it behind her ear. They stared lovingly at each other as he took her hands in his and planted soft kisses on the backs of her fingers.

Turning over Marianna's hands, Martak gently placed a kiss in each of her palms, then pressed them against his own, sealing their love. Ten fingers touched as their lips sought what their hearts desired.

Martak swept Marianna into his powerful arms. He was alive and she felt his every muscle scream for her as his strong, gentle pressure overtook the edges of her being. While the flames slowly turned to embers, the fire between them grew, and he made love to her with the intensity of life-affirming passion that comes from surviving life-threatening danger.

Long before dawn, the lovers awoke with their bodies entwined. They smiled at each other and then began to speak simultaneously in hushed tones. Marianna wanted to know everything that had occurred the day before, and Martak tried to explain all that had transpired. There was a brief pause before they both started anew and interrupted one another again. They laughed.

Marianna let him tell his story while she prepared her morning cup of tea. In detail, Martak described his meeting with the King and the failed attempt on his life, never taking his eyes from Marianna's graceful hands as she stirred the brew. Moving the spoon in slow circles, Marianna quickly grasped the significance of the King's wishes, the danger facing the Princess and Martak's reluctance to accept the mission, while shuddering at the thought of an assassin lying in wait for him.

Taking his handsome face between her warm hands and looking deeply into his searching eyes, Marianna spoke the words of love and encouragement that Martak needed to hear. "My beloved, you must make this voyage. You must save the Princess from Evil and protect the Kingdom. I know with all my heart and soul that you can succeed. The sea creatures will lead you in the waters during the day and the stars will guide you at night."

Martak regarded Marianna with wonder. Her words gave meaning to the decision he had already made. Bolstered by her support, fortified with her blessing and empowered with the strength of the love they shared, he returned to the palace and accepted the mission, swearing allegiance to King, country and the forces of Good.

Chapter Thirteen

THE MOON

The King was grateful for Martak's response, but worried by the passing of precious time. He ordered the swiftest vessel in the royal fleet to be manned by a loyal crew committed to undertaking the dangerous mission.

By nightfall, the black and gold ship, armed for battle, prepared to set sail. Marianna joined the few granted permission to watch the secret expedition's departure. As the banner emblazoned with the King's coat of arms was hoisted above the mainmast, Martak grabbed a rope and swung out from the ship to find his beloved, who was straining to catch a final glimpse of him.

He led her to a quiet spot and pointed at the full moon. "Only one moon circles the earth," he whispered. "When you miss me, look at the moon and know that wherever I am, I am watching it too, and thinking of you. Our thoughts will transcend the Heavens, and we will be connected through the glow of moonlight."

Embracing each other, requited love burst forth from their hearts, bathing them in their own radiance. They shared a last passionate kiss and then he was gone, only the warmth of his breath lingering on her lips.

Clutching her aching heart, Marianna stood on the dock until the ship passed from sight. Waves of anguish swept over her as she thought of her beloved, not knowing the dangers he faced or the fate of her dear Princess. She continued to gaze at the moon, and it became even more luminescent and began to gently waver. As the vibrations fell into synch with her heartbeat, she knew she had reached him and was comforted.

Martak leaned over the rail of the ship. The salt spray misted his face as he inhaled the scent of the sea. Staring up at the moon, he sensed the gentle wavering of lunar beams and felt connected with Marianna. He thought, *The moon controls the tide and our love is stronger than the never-ending rhythm of the sea. My love for Marianna will be my guiding star, my true north.*

No matter what lay ahead, the fates had decreed this was a journey that must be taken. He smiled confidently and headed to his cabin for a good night's sleep and dreams of his beloved.

Chapter Fourteen

THE SEA DRAGON

As the sun trailed the moon across the sky and waves lashed against the ship, Martak was jolted from a sound sleep by the first mate's shouting.

"Martak, Martak! Quick! Look to starboard."

He bounded out of bed and raced to the deck.

Roaring toward his vessel was an immense, three-headed sea dragon. Long tendrils of fire snaked from two of its gray-green, one-eyed heads, threatening all who passed the shoals of its lair on the notorious Ponderous Rocks. Martak had heard of this demon from his Guide. According to lore, the lonely beast terrorized sailors out of boredom and meant no harm despite its ferocity, but was that really true? Never did Martak imagine the real horror of its appearance or the sounds blaring from the third head situated between the two fiery bookends.

As the sea dragon's tail encircled the ship and his heads swirled around the deck, jaws parted to incinerate, the crew cringed before their fate.

The dragon would be upon them in moments. Martak quickly considered his strategic options. They could not outrun the beast, and there was not enough time to maneuver the ship broadside and ready the cannons for firing.

As the dragon neared the ship, Martak noticed that the noise pouring from the creature was music, as if singing were propelling it through the water. *We can stand and brutally fight a fire-breathing dragon, but there's a good chance we will be doomed and fail to fulfill our mission,* he considered. *What should I do?*

Then it came to him—something Marianna had told him one afternoon when they were together in the woods. Lying with his head in her lap and gazing at the sky, he listened to her sing and his heart was at peace with the world. Sensing that in him, she said, "Dearest one, the love in my voice will be with you always, so if ever you are in danger and music can save you, sing the words I tell you now."

Martak thought, *Should I try it? Should I risk it? If we wait until the dragon is close enough to hear my voice, and that fails, there will be no choice but to fight to the death.* Martak ordered his men to arm themselves for battle as he ran to the highest mast and climbed it with the agility and determination of a hungry jaguar closing in on its next meal. As the ship rocked and swayed, Martak stared the dragon straight in its three eyes, took a deep breath, unleashed his powerful tenor and cast his beloved's lyrics into harm's way.

Now, as the beast closed in on Martak's vessel, it heard a sound that confused it. What was the source? Who was singing those strange words? All three of the dragon's heads shared the same thought simultaneously, the first time they had ever thought as one. Straight ahead, the creature saw a man at the very top of the tallest mast, his hands cupped to his mouth and singing. The dragon drew closer to the ship, mesmerized by the voice.

Martak continued to bellow a musical refrain at the top of his lungs, singing his heart out in blind faith to his love as the dragon drew nearer. Unsure of its effect, he sang even louder and more fervently. When the sea dragon was upon the vessel, Martak saw that its three heads were now working as one, and the beast was moving to the rhythm of Martak's tune. *Could it be?* he thought.

Armed with swords and daggers, axes and clubs, the royal sailors bravely prepared to defend their lives and the black and gold ship. Even so, as the sea dragon's tail encircled the ship and his heads swirled around the deck, jaws parted to incinerate, the crew cringed before their fate. Then, much like a child expecting a smack receives a kiss instead, the sailors' eyes widened in disbelief. Rather than searing flames, they were bathed in the most delightful music. Inspired by Martak's rich tenor, the three-headed sea dragon listened to his melody and then blended his refrain into its own perfect, three-part harmony. The serenade went on for hours, and as the sun set, the dragon safely escorted the black and gold ship to the farthest boundaries of the creature's range.

The danger averted, Martak's eyes were drawn to the Heavens. Gazing at the moon, he felt connected to Marianna. His heart was filled with gratitude, love and longing for his beloved. Moonlight gently illuminated the ship as Martak headed below to sleep and dream about Marianna and the first time their love merged by the brook.

Chapter Fifteen

THE STOWAWAY

Loud and vigorous pounding on his cabin door awakened Martak.

Whack! "Ow!" he yelled as he bolted upright from sleep and the warming tingle of a nearly fulfilled dream. Having just banged his head on the timber of a vessel quite different from the one he had been preparing to board, Martak rubbed his head and sighed. *Why is it that every time my quiet thoughts come to the brink of passion, one or another of this crew finds some way to interrupt us?*

"Martak, hurry, come at once to the hold!" shouted the anxious voice from the hallway.

"What alarms you?" he called back, but the sailor was already gone.

Sighing again at the unfulfilled desires of his dream, Martak bounded down the ladder leading to the ship's hold, wondering how much worse it could be than yesterday's fire-breathing, singing sea monster. But something was clearly amiss because, while making his descent, he saw no one. When he reached the hold, he froze. The entire royal crew knelt in a circle, staring in shock and disbelief, at the most unexpected—and uninvited—passenger.

It was Rosy. Princess Rosy. Princess Rosalind Cordelia Theresa Miranda Victoria. There she stood, Her Royal Majesty-To-Be. Arms crossed defiantly. Lips pouting regally. Eyes scrunched. A freshly discovered, frightened stowaway.

"Rosy, what are you doing here?" he blurted, abandoning her title and addressing her as if she were any child in need of his attention.

Rosy loved that Martak called her by name whenever he accompanied her and Marianna on walks. The familiarity made her feel like Martak was the older brother she had always wished for, but at this precise moment, she knew that unless she maintained her royal bearing, she would break into frightened sobs in front of everyone. Posing in imitation of the Queen on state occasions, head proud and erect, she regally spouted, "How dare you address the Princess of the land in such a manner."

Martak instantly realized the Princess's delicate state and that she would fall to pieces if he continued talking to her as he had. Instead, he dropped to his knee and in a courtly manner exclaimed, "I beg your pardon, my Princess. I was so surprised at seeing you that I forgot my place. Please forgive me."

Like one who fires a gun with blanks and unexpectedly sees the target fall, Rosy was caught unaware and unsure of what to do next. *Could he really be letting me get away with this?* she wondered. Keeping up with the royal role-play, the Princess stood even taller. "I forgive you, but don't ever do it again," she continued imperiously. "This is a royal ship, and I have the right to be here. Now, please rise."

As he stood up, Martak's irritation with this little charade rose as well.

"Princess, permit me to take you up to the main cabin so I may apprise you of the nature of our voyage." Before the Princess could deliver another line in her little play, Martak's very strong hand was around her small arm, and he firmly "escorted" her up the ladder. Showing wisdom far beyond her years, no further words came from the royal mouth until they were alone.

Martak just stared at her with puzzlement, and she stared back stubbornly.

"You're mad at me, aren't you, Martak?"

"Mad? Me? Master of the Forest, tamer of sea dragons, handpicked emissary of the King and protector of good? Mad? No, Princess, I'm not mad." Tightening his hand into a fist as he said those words, Martak really wanted to tell her he was so angry, he could scream. But his self-control was such that he resisted the temptation.

Martak went on quietly, deliberately, and with all the patience he could muster. "Let me put this very simply. I am on a special assignment for the King. Your being here is a problem. Caring for you will distract my crew from their duties, and risks our mission and the safety of the Kingdom that we are sworn to protect," he explained, while moving his head closer and closer to hers until he was talking directly into her face. Then pushing back his chair and standing, Martak continued with concern. "Don't you think your absence from the palace will frighten those who love you, like your parents and Marianna? They must be terribly worried. How could you run away? What were you thinking?"

"Pleeease, Martak," she pleaded, fidgeting in her seat. "You're making this sound like I did something really bad. This is just a boat ride. I left a note for Mother and Father on my bed and I'm sure they told Marianna."

Martak let her prattle on. How could he tell her the real reason for this journey was to protect her from the Evil that threatened her personally, as well as all that was good in the Kingdom? That neither she nor the Kingdom were safe until she reached her eighth birthday.

There was no time to turn the ship around and return her to the palace. The mission came first, but Martak's instincts for danger were sharp and on high alert.

Before the ship set sail, the King had anointed Martak with a blessing, proclaiming him the "Princess's Deliverer." Would these royal words now come to haunt them? His mind churned with questions. *How can Rosy be here? Who or what is behind this?*

She interrupted his thoughts with an impish grin that brought out her dimples as she cheerfully teased, "Martak, guess what? Yesterday while I was hiding in the bottom of the ship, I heard such beautiful music. Do you think whoever was singing could do it again?"

Martak just looked at her, smiled, and shook his head, while Rosy scampered back down to the hold in search of the alluring melody.

Chapter Sixteen

EVIL

Martak assessed the situation. Having the Princess on board was not good and certainly made things more complicated. He pondered how this could have happened. *Suppose she had not left a note—after all, she is unreliable. By now, they're probably turning the Kingdom upside down looking for her. And what of Marianna? What state must she be in? Even on a good day she worries about the Princess. Maybe she will be blamed for Rosy's disappearance.* Troubling thoughts raced through his mind as he sought to form a plan.

He could not take the child home. There was no time and the sky threatened a mounting storm. However, he could dispatch one of the ship's skiffs with a courier to carry word to the palace. Martak asked for a volunteer to risk returning with a message for the court, and found one in a weathered old sea hand who had survived many adventures.

The sailor departed quickly to let the King and Queen know that their daughter was safe at sea. But then again, was she really safe? In his heart, Martak was not sure, but he was duty bound to protect her. At least she was under his watchful eye while the fate of Evil's curse played out.

The ship continued onward as the sky darkened, clouds roiled, thunder cracked and lightning split the air. Torrential rains poured from the Heavens and the winds howled, raising violent waves that crashed onto the deck. The black and gold ship, alone at sea, tossed for hours. Even experienced sailors felt ill as the ship rocked and swayed. Rosy had never felt so sick in her entire life and regretted her impulsive decision to return to the hold in search of the mysterious melody. But unbeknownst to her or others, forces beyond her control had compelled her to do so.

Martak found Rosy doubled over on the floor of the hold. He gathered the nauseated child in his arms and carried her to his cabin, now designated the royal quarters. After tucking her into bed, he left with his belongings to bunk with the crew.

By morning, the storm had moved on and the sea was placid again. Those on board began to feel better, although Rosy still looked a little green. That day and the next, Martak and the sailors searched the coastline for clues that would lead them to the source of Evil and liberate Rosy—and indeed all of them—from the forces of darkness.

Martak noticed that Rosy continued to look wan. Color had deserted her normally pink cheeks, and she seemed lost in her own world. He was accustomed to seeing her bounce around and make others laugh with goofy songs and impersonations, but now she was withdrawn and uncommunicative, as if in a trance. The sea had remained calm, so there was no logical explanation for her strange appearance and behavior. Martak's observations disturbed him.

The following day, while much of the crew launched skiffs to explore the shoreline in search of Evil, Martak kept an attentive watch on Rosy. She barely ate breakfast before disappearing again into the dimly lit hold. He quietly followed, but was unprepared for what he found. Rosy stood in the middle of the room with outstretched arms, swaying to a slow, rhythmic melody. The tempo rapidly increased, and the enticing refrain blurred together until all that could be heard was a whirring sound. Rosy twirled faster and faster as if caught in a whirlpool. She spun uncontrollably, and with each movement grew weaker and more unsteady. Martak called to her, but she could not hear him or acknowledge his voice. When the whirring reached a high-pitched crescendo, she fell exhausted to the floor. Martak quickly picked her up and carried her to the deck, handling her as gently as a newborn fawn.

In the sunlight, Rosy looked almost dead and Martak began to understand the horror of what he had witnessed. He held her tightly, hoping some of his own strength would transfer to her fragile form.

"Tell me what happened," Martak whispered to Rosy.

In a barely audible voice she confessed. "I love the music. It speaks to me."

"Tell me about the music."

"In the bottom of the ship. It's so beautiful," she replied.

"What do you hear?" he probed gently.

"A song," she responded, her eyes glazed.

"Rosy, dear Princess, what are the words? Sing the song for me," as no words had been apparent to Martak.

For the first time, she turned to look up at him, struggling to focus on his face, and nodded. With a half smile, she began chanting to a haunting tune.

"Be with me
Out at sea
We will play mer-ri-ly.

We'll dance and sing
To please the King
Oh so very mer-ri-ly."

Martak finally grasped the meaning of the bizarre behavior that Rosy had been unable to control. While he and his men searched up and down the coastline for the source of the curse, Evil turned siren had been hiding in their midst. While he and his crew were serenaded by the three-headed sea dragon, Evil was seducing this child with its own deceitful melody and ensnaring her with words that only she could hear. Martak turned to steel at the thought of this malevolent presence on his ship—a presence sadistic enough to tempt a child to her death by luring her with what she loved most. Now beyond anger, Martak was ready to kill.

Martak had discovered the true treachery of Evil, and it was beyond even the King's worst fears. Rosy was the Keeper of the Flame of Innocence. He intuited that her death by Evil's manipulation would end all that Good represented, and all that was innocent in the Kingdom would perish along with her. This was more than a curse—this was an attempt to destroy her, whether or not she touched the golden, iridescent globe. For if she were to die, Evil's presence also would continue to grow unchecked.

Martak fought his rage and tried to recall what his Guide had taught him about sirens so long ago. But he could not remember. He had only the remainder of the day to recall the lesson. Rosy would turn eight years old at midnight.

Chapter Seventeen

DESTINY

Clutching the pallid, fading child in his arms, Martak stood at the bow of his ship and stared into the glassy water. His thoughts flowed unfocused. *Is this the last day this child shall ever see? If Evil plots so cunningly to kill such innocence, then must there not be some greater power, a greater good so threatening to Evil that treachery like this is its only recourse?*

Martak's thoughts trailed off as his eyes were drawn into the depths of the sea. Before him, a pool of agitated water spiraled upward, and he heard an inner voice speaking to him.

"Martak, you stand at the brink of your destiny." The voice echoed throughout his being. "From birth, your life was entrusted to one who swore an oath to guide your special gifts and prepare you for this moment when the forces of Good and Evil would battle for the future of innocence. Trust what you have learned. Trust what you love."

Clutching the pallid, fading child in his arms, Martak stood at the bow of his ship and stared into the glassy water.

Then he saw her—Marianna's image rising from the circular rippling in the sea. Martak shouted out to her with the force of a warrior's cry. "My beloved, you have shown me the joy that true love brings to life. Now, help me save the life of the Princess."

He envisioned Marianna's slender fingers slowly stirring her tea, the spoon in her hand going round and round. He stared at the image of his love in the swirling waters. "That's it!" he exclaimed, understanding at last and so excited he nearly dropped Rosy.

Amid the horror of witnessing Princess Rosy's wild spinning toward her death, Martak had overlooked his own encounters with mysterious whirling in the glen and at the forest's edge. But Marianna had pointed him to a common thread connecting these incidents.

The whirring sound that accompanied Rosy's wild spinning was the same noise he had heard after both unsuccessful attempts on his own life. Aside from the would-be assassins, the only other presence during both those attempts was the Shadowmaker.

With this realization, everything fell into place for Martak, and he now understood the reason for the attacks. He and Rosy were being threatened by the same evil force. Evil knew that Martak's Guide was Good's chosen warrior, and Martak was being groomed to be his Guide's successor. Martak, therefore, was also Evil's enemy and must be destroyed. Finding Martak alone and distracted by his thoughts, Evil seized these rare opportunities to slay his young adversary through his ruthless agent, the Shadowmaker.

A mantling sense of power and purpose came over Martak, for now he understood his destiny. He saw his enemy clearly and swore to the Heavens that he—and Good—would prevail.

Martak held Rosy tightly. As long as the child was with him, he knew he could protect her. But wary of Evil's trickery and deceit, he also realized that the Princess and all that Good stood for were not truly safe until Rosy's eighth birthday passed without incident.

Under his direction and watchful eye, the crew spent the rest of the day scouring every inch of the ship for any trace of Evil. They found nothing.

Chapter Eighteen

REVELATION

No sooner had the sun set than the moon climbed in the night sky. It seemed so far away, and yet its presence gave enormous comfort to Martak, for it linked him to Marianna and brought her clearly into focus. He wanted so much to tell her about all that had transpired. That he had discovered his destiny, that he understood the enormity of his task, and that he was determined to triumph for her sake, for Rosy's and for all of the Kingdom.

Staring at the moon, he silently shared his heartfelt thoughts and prayed that Marianna would receive his message. He asked her blessing for the measures he would need to take to protect the Princess in the coming hours and thanked the Heavens for having brought Marianna into his life. He wanted her to know that he would return once his destiny was fulfilled, never to leave her side again. Forever after, she would be his reason for being.

With only a few hours remaining until midnight and Rosy's birthday, Martak's thoughts turned again to strategy. He mentally reviewed the battlefield, lining up the players in Evil's insidious plot to destroy innocence and supplant Good.

There were the dark forces—Evil in his various incarnations and his minions, led by the Shadowmaker. On the other side were the forces of Good—his Guide, Princess Rosy, Marianna, the King and Queen, his mother and father.

Martak was startled by his own thoughts. "Mother? Father?" he questioned out loud. What did they have to do with this?

His breathing quickened as the truth dawned on him. The fateful events on board the ship were not unrelated to his birth. Struggling with the magnitude of what he now knew to be true, Martak's heart ached for the parents he had never known.

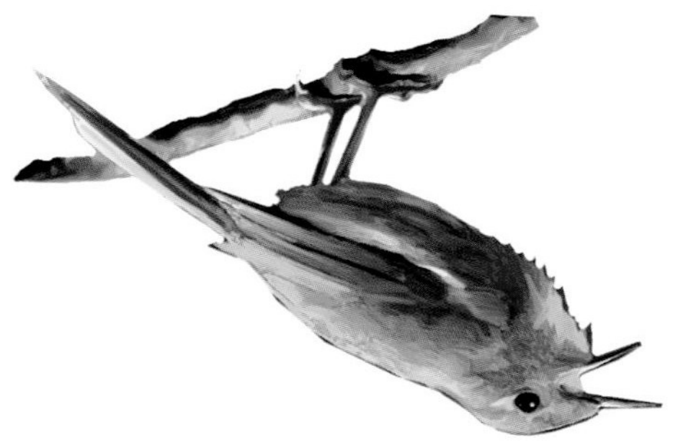

Chapter Nineteen

A Child is Born

Martak wondered what had happened to his parents, but his Guide never spoke of them. When he was young, he often asked about his mother and father. His Guide always offered the same response with patience and kindness. "Their love is the reason you are here. There is no more to say."

In truth, his parents were at the core of the epic battle between Good and Evil that began before his birth. Less than a year after that fateful night when two lovers reached for the golden, iridescent globe, a boy was born to them. His birth filled his parents with the profound light of joy—a light that enabled them to make an agonizing decision when Good came to them bearing news of Evil's trickery and the danger their newborn faced. Good explained the nature of the curse that threatened their son's life and that of a second child, should they have one.

The parents' uncontrollable grief in learning of the bitter fate brought upon them and their son did not shake their unyielding faith in Good. Still, it was with great reluctance and only because his life was in danger that they entrusted their newborn son to Good's care and guiding hand.

Good hoped to hide the child before Evil learned of the birth and plotted the boy's destruction. To protect their son, Martak's parents could never reveal his existence. Fortunately, his mother was a private woman who had kept her pregnancy a secret and, being robust, her swollen belly had been hidden under layers of simple garments.

Time passed and Martak's parents were mindful that the powers of Good stood by to look after their son, and that his well-being was entrusted to Good's bravest warrior, the man who became his Guide. But even this knowledge did not diminish the ever-present sadness in their lives. They could have another child, but the thought of being separated from a second child—even for only eight years while the curse remained a threat—was so overwhelming that they could not bring themselves to try.

One crisp fall evening, as the couple walked near the edge of the forest, a delicate songbird grazed the mother's hand, beckoning them to a small pool. Peering into the shallow water, the lovers saw an image of their beautiful boy at play in the woods. Their profound joy at unexpectedly seeing him was tempered with the sorrow of not being able to hold him or know the pleasure of raising him. Overcome, Martak's mother clutched her husband and sobbed with bittersweet anguish. "My precious son, I love you, and I miss you so very much."

Martak's parents ached for their beloved son. While they could see he was a happy child, it did not diminish the emptiness they felt. Indeed, in time, that powerful image of Martak would alter their lives.

Chapter Twenty

Quest for the Princess

Back at the palace, things were not going well. Princess Rosy had disappeared and the Kingdom was in chaos. The King and Queen were frantic. Their beloved daughter, whom they had protected for almost eight years, was missing only days before her most significant birthday. They feared that Evil lurked everywhere. They prayed for her safe return and that Martak would succeed in protecting her from the curse, never dreaming he was now fighting to save her life.

And Marianna? She was beside herself with worry and anxiety. The royals did not blame her for Rosy's disappearance. Marianna's love for and devotion to the child were well known. Since the day of the horrifying game of hide-and-seek when the Princess had run away, Marianna never left her royal charge unattended while she was in her care.

> *Tanner saw something quite wonderful in the stranger's hand—a small wooden chest with polished brass hinges.*

Meanwhile, the old sailor who had volunteered to deliver the news of Rosy's whereabouts never made it back to the royal harbor. His small craft crashed on a treacherous reef and sank during the raging storm. Fortunately, the seaman survived the wreckage and swam to shore, finding refuge in a cave on the Ponderous Rocks, where he awaited rescue.

Rosy's claim that she had left a note for her parents was true but somewhat misleading. When the Princess arose the morning of Martak's departure, it was a glorious day. The sun was shining and her adventurous spirit drew her outdoors as the day beckoned. She impulsively decided to skip her lessons and go for one of her secret walks outside the palace, in search of Tanner, her playmate in the village.

Using her best handwriting, she printed a note that read "Gon fur wak. Be bak soon," and left it on her bed, assuming that the servants would find it and give it to her parents or Marianna. Exceptionally proud of acting so responsibly, she donned one of her plainer dresses and set out with a smile for an early-morning stroll. Skipping merrily around the palace, she waved to the guards posted at every doorway. As she approached the entrance to the servants' quarters, the young guard stationed there was so engrossed in flirting with a brazen maid that neither noticed the Princess as she slipped by them.

What Rosy never anticipated was the gentle breeze that blew in through an open window, carrying the note off her bed and depositing it under her commodious, hand-painted armoire. A quick inspection of her room by the servants offered no clue to her disappearance. It was only after a thorough search of her private quarters by castle guards, who wrestled the heavy furniture aside to check beneath, that the note was discovered. By then, she was long gone.

Rosy sneaked out of the palace using one of the secret passages she knew so well. It led to an opening near the village where she saw her friend, Tanner. Before she could get his attention, however, Rosy noticed a peculiar-looking man in a cloak approach him, and she instinctively sought cover behind a thicket of shrubs. Hidden from sight, she witnessed a most unusual scenario.

The stranger hailed Tanner, interrupting his play. Unafraid, though mindful of his parents' admonition about talking to strangers, the boy ignored the intruder. But the stranger persisted, calling Tanner by name. The boy turned defiantly and, with all the bravado he could muster, demanded, "How do you know my name?"

"Everyone knows your name," the stranger replied. "Your bravery and athletic skills have made you a legend among the children in this village." The flattery had the desired effect and Tanner relaxed, enabling the stranger to come closer.

Tanner saw something quite wonderful in the stranger's hand as he neared—a small wooden chest with mysterious carvings and polished brass hinges. The boy could not take his eyes from the box. Inching closer, the stranger said, "Come, take it. It contains a gift for you, with great power that will be yours." Taking the chest from the stranger, the boy opened it and beheld a round, glowing ball that magically grew bigger and bigger before his eyes.

The boy was entranced, exclaiming, "For me?" Grinning from ear to ear with the innocence of youth, he eagerly reached for the golden, iridescent globe.

As the boy embraced the glowing form, the stranger burst into a diabolical laugh so startling that the youth jumped back, thinking him mad. But the laughter was short-lived. As the stranger stood wide-eyed in disbelief, Tanner began to enthusiastically kick, bounce and then throw the ball against a stone wall. Enjoying his new toy, the boy grasped a large stick and tossed the ball in the air. As he coiled to bat the object, the mortified stranger hollered, "Stop! Stop!"

"Watch me," the boy replied as he uncoiled, keeping his eye on the glowing form. The stranger could only moan at what was about to happen to his precious object. He raced toward it at the very instant a perfect swing brought stick and ball together with a resounding *whakkkkk*. The globe flew directly at the charging stranger, who caught it in a most unintended manner and painful place. As the stranger lay writhing on the ground, the boy came running over.

"Sorrryyyyy! Are you all right?" he inquired apologetically.

All pretense of charm now gone, the stranger ordered the boy to go, but Tanner just stood there. Clutching the orb and still bent in pain, Evil's servant limped away, having failed his master and fearful of the consequences.

As soon as the stranger was gone, Rosy rushed over to Tanner. While sometimes he found her annoying, now he was happy to see her familiar face. They walked together in the direction of the sea, talking animatedly about his encounter with the stranger.

When they reached the harbor, they immediately saw the dock swarming with people, making it difficult to observe what was happening. They climbed a hill to get a better view and then huddled behind a stone wall. Straining their necks to peer over the wall, they were excited to see the bustling activity as those below readied a mighty black and gold ship for battle.

Royal soldiers patrolled the wharf while experienced crewmen loaded provisions and weapons aboard the ship. The dock was crowded with large wooden chests, crates, barrels and other containers filled with items for an imminent voyage.

Much to her surprise, Rosy recognized Martak standing on the deck and barking out orders. Overcome with delight at seeing him and realizing he was about to set sail, she quickly turned to Tanner.

"I really need to go," she blurted. Acting impulsively, Rosy ran around the wall and toward the ship, leaving Tanner dumbstruck and confused. As she disappeared among the heavy cargo stacked along the quay, Tanner turned and headed home alone, absorbed in kicking stones.

What he failed to notice lurking nearby was the Shadowmaker, who also had witnessed the exchange between Tanner and the girl, as well as her sprint to the ship. Evil's agent sped from the scene to report to his master.

Evil knew from his spies that a boy named Tanner had been born to the lovers, who had touched the globe, and freed him to roam the Kingdom many years ago. Although one child was not cause for great concern—as he had until a second child turned eight to entice either child to embrace the globe—Evil decided there was no point in delaying his eventual triumph. He dispatched one of his underlings, globe in hand, to find Tanner and lure him into touching the glowing object.

Evil was certain he had outwitted Good. His days of risking permanent banishment would soon be over and his dream to rule the Kingdom would be fulfilled.

Now, news of the day's events sent Evil into an uncontrollable rage. Pacing violently back and forth, his mind raced with furious thoughts. *How could the child of those lovers embrace the globe without unleashing my full powers? Why is the Kingdom not shrouded in darkness? Tanner is the wrong child!* Cursing the Heavens, Evil realized there must be another child or perhaps other children at large. Livid, he summoned his forces and demanded that they scour the Kingdom for other possible children of the lovers. But the search would uncover no such offspring in the land.

Meanwhile, the distraught King and Queen ordered their own search of every inch of the Kingdom to find Princess Rosalind Cordelia Theresa Miranda Victoria, Keeper of the Flame of Innocence. The reward for her safe return was a lifetime of riches and a place at court.

When the Shadowmaker brought word to his master of the palace's frantic search for the missing Princess and reported that he had seen a young girl running to a ship in the harbor, Evil knew at once the girl must be the missing Princess. She was the key to his destiny, and he must find her and soon, before time and his opportunity ran out.

Chapter Twenty-One

The Abduction

Marianna was obsessed with finding her precious Princess. She cared nothing about the reward, wanting only to know that Rosy was safe and that she would be able to take the child into her arms and hug and kiss her again. Marianna combed the castle grounds every day, relentlessly seeking clues to Rosy's disappearance.

Walking in a direction opposite her accustomed path with the Princess, Marianna ventured into an unfamiliar area of the palace grounds and found herself at the Knights' Training Center. She surveyed where brave soldiers honed their skills in preparation for tournaments and future battles by practicing horsemanship and combat with swords and lances. It was a complete military facility, and, even in her troubled state, she marveled at the equipment on display.

The training center initially appeared deserted since hundreds of knights and most of the King's army had volunteered to search for the missing Princess. Every soldier loyal to the King was committed to finding Rosy. As Marianna made her way through the facility, a few knights who remained to protect the palace halted their activities to chivalrously greet the lovely lady in their midst.

In her anxiety, Marianna did not stop to acknowledge the knights' attention, or even notice the way they stared unabashedly at her beauty. She also failed to observe one of them lurking in the shadows—a large figure with thick, dark hair and a black beard. He was dressed in black armor and glared at her with a menacing glint. Always a troublemaker, the rogue had never seen such a gorgeous creature and he wanted the wench for himself.

Exhausted by her fruitless search and with the day waning, Marianna finally abandoned her effort and headed home to her parents' cottage in the village. Still anxious and wracked by fear for Rosy's safety, she trudged home, preoccupied with thoughts of the missing Princess and the horrible things that might have befallen her.

As she reached the village, Marianna came upon a group of five children playing blind man's bluff. Interrupting their game, she implored, "Have any of you seen the missing Princess?"

They looked at her and then at each other. Some said no outright, while others just shrugged their shoulders and shook their heads. Then it occurred to Marianna that these children might never have seen the Princess, so she showed them a miniature painting of Rosy, a gift from the King and Queen that she always carried in her pocket.

She was shocked by their simultaneous expressions of surprise. "W-we know that girl, b-but we didn't know she w-was the P-Princess!" stammered one of the younger boys. "Honest, w-we didn't know."

"Sometimes she plays with us," another boy chimed in. "She's funny! Is that really the Princess?"

"She doesn't dress like a princess, all fancy and that," volunteered the only girl present.

Pointing to Tanner, the village bully taunted, "Why don't you ask him? She likes him!"

Marianna approached Tanner, who had stepped away from the group and, with downcast eyes, was toeing the ground in search of a stone to kick.

"Tanner, look at me," Marianna insisted, lifting his chin so he was forced to meet her gaze. "Do you know where the Princess is?" she demanded. "We need to find her. You must tell me anything you know of her whereabouts."

Tanner gulped. "She's just a girl who shows up and plays with us. How were we supposed to know she was the Princess?"

"Tanner, you and your friends have done nothing wrong," Marianna reassured him. "Just tell me when you last saw the Princess."

"Well…um…um…the day we saw the big, black and gold ship in the harbor."

"The day you saw the ship in the harbor?" Marianna repeated in disbelief. "What were you doing there?"

"We weren't doing anything, just watching and then she ran to the ship."

"Who ran to the ship?"

"The girl, I mean the Princess!"

"Is the Princess on the ship? Did you see her get on it?" Tanner was a husky boy, but Marianna was ready to shake him to his core to get the full story out of him.

"I'm not sure. She saw the man who walks with you standing on the deck and she just ran toward him. I don't know what happened after that. I needed to get home, so I left."

"Tanner, is there anything else you can tell me about that day?"

"No ma'am. Honest. I've told you everything I know."

Marianna's head spun with this revelation. She was heartened to think the Princess was with Martak, but apprehensive that the child was sailing into danger. She had to tell the King and Queen what she had learned and as quickly as possible. Turning from the village, she ran toward the palace. Despite her sense of urgency, Marianna could not maintain the fast pace. She slowed to a walk and then halted altogether, hands on her knees, to catch her breath.

Lost in her apprehension and gasping for air, Marianna was caught off guard when a pair of arms seized her roughly from behind and plunged her into her own nightmare. She fought back, yelling and kicking, scratching and biting her abductor, but she was no match for the Black Knight, who had stalked her from the time she left the palace and now carried her toward the nearby forest. The harder she worked to twist free of his grip, the tighter he held her, and when he put his hand over her mouth and nose to quiet her, she feared she would suffocate. But that was not his intent. When her frantic behavior quieted down, he removed his hand because he did not want to kill her before taking the opportunity to pleasure himself. Holding a knife to her neck, he warned her that if she made a sound, he would slit her throat, and they silently made their way deeper into the forest.

Marianna was terrified, but, unbeknownst to her, she was not alone.

Prior to setting sail on the King's mission, Martak had called together the animals in his forest kingdom—the large and small, young and old, quick and slow. "I am leaving on a special assignment," he told them. "I ask all of you, my friends, to watch over Marianna while I am gone. No harm must come to her."

Since they loved their master and knew how much he adored his beloved, the woodland creatures stood ready to obey. Although he never would have asked it of them, each one pledged to protect her, even if it meant giving up its life. On this, they were in unanimous agreement.

Ever since Martak's departure, Marianna had been under their watchful eyes. Birds always fluttered nearby, while smaller animals followed her along footpaths. She enjoyed the wildlife but never questioned the reason for their constant companionship.

Now the creatures moved decisively to action. News of Marianna's abduction spread quickly through the forest and the Council of Carnivores, the fiercer beasts, assembled to assess the peril and formulate a rescue plan.

Meanwhile, the Black Knight and Marianna reached a place deep in the forest where his horse stood. He sat Marianna against a tree and tied her hands behind it. No sooner had the tormentor turned his back than a little bunny darted from the underbrush, and Marianna soon felt it feverishly gnawing the ropes. Her heart was beating out of control, but she was comforted by the bunny's warmth and its earnest attempt to help bolstered her courage. She had to get free, both for her own sake and for the sake of the Princess. She had to reach the King and Queen.

Marianna focused her wits on saving herself. *I must make him see me as a person and not a victim*, she thought. She tried talking to the Knight, but he only leered—he was not interested in conversation and told her to keep quiet. Swallowing hard and taking a deep breath, she attempted to speak to him again, which only angered him more. The villain raised his hand to strike her across the face. As he began the downward swing of his arm, there was a cry and a thunderous beating of hundreds of birds' wings swarming behind him, like the roar of raging winds. He turned in the direction of the deafening noise while he swung and Marianna ducked. His hand cracked against the tree instead of her cheek.

Stinging with pain and frustration, the Knight was wild with fury. He easily could have pushed her to the ground and taken her there, but decided to abandon the forest for his own castle, where he could serve his licentious pleasure at his leisure. Half dragging, half lifting her onto the saddle, he mounted the horse behind her and galloped away.

The Black Knight's castle loomed large and threatening. Two burly guardsmen greeted their master and roughly led Marianna to the dungeon, shoving her into a decayed, cold cell. Alone and shivering in the darkness, she ran the palms of her hands along the damp floor and reached along the moldy walls, searching for an opening or any possible means of escape. There was none.

Trapped deep inside the castle, Marianna did not feel the ground quaking or hear the clamor as the creatures under Martak's command charged in full fury, determined to rescue her. Fearlessly, the larger beasts leaped into the moat while animals that could not swim grasped their backs. Despite their heroic efforts, neither claws nor hoofs could scale the impenetrable wall surrounding the castle. Retreating to the bank, baring teeth and snarling with rage, the four-legged battalion raced back and forth, searching for a way to storm the fortress.

The guards returned to Marianna's cell at nightfall and carried her, fighting and screaming, to a strange room that was very cold and reeked with the scent of hostile animals.

As two severe-looking women, silent and emotionless, peeled off Marianna's dirty gown and bathed her, she realized they were not alone. Eyes watched them from the shadows. Cold gray eyes, steel-blue eyes, intense green eyes—all fastened on her and following her every move. Any attempt to break loose from the matrons, or a step in any direction, would bring her within reach of vicious wolves standing ready to pounce. There was no escape from this den.

The matrons cloaked Marianna in a magnificent white robe edged with golden threads and the guards returned to take her to their master's quarters. Marianna's heart was pounding and her insides churned as fear and disbelief washed over her. Her eyes scanned the narrow corridor for a way to flee. Seeing none, she turned on the guard behind her and fiercely pounded his chest, but he easily pinned her wrists and held onto them as he propelled her forward. Still, she refused to accept the hopelessness of her situation and entered the Black Knight's bedchamber with the regal bearing of a queen, and displaying outright hostility toward her captors. Whatever happened, she was determined to retain her dignity and self-control.

The Knight's bedroom was large and darkly paneled, with massive arches pointing to the ceiling. Hundreds of candles in bizarre and twisted shapes lit the room, casting eerie shadows in all directions. A large, freshly made bed with deep pillows dominated the space and the guards clumsily threw her onto it, fighting their own lust as they tied her hands to the headboard. They hoped she would be turned over to them once their master discarded her.

The Black Knight appeared soon after the guards' reluctant exit. Even he was startled by Marianna's exquisite beauty. In the glow of candlelight, she radiated an ethereal presence and he approached her, intrigued. He sat on the edge of the bed by her side and slowly ran his fingers through her hair, which rippled across the pillows. The back of his coarse hand stroked her delicate face. The evil predator was in no rush to bring the night to a close.

Repulsed, Marianna turned away as he continued to slide his hand down her throat and over her robed body. Holding her breath, gritting her teeth, she froze at his touch. Enjoying her humiliation and how easy she was to manipulate, his fingers sought her delicate skin and he slipped his hand under the robe. As she arched and twisted, trying to withdraw from the pressure of his palm, her eyes were drawn to a window and the sight of the moon glowing in the night sky. She screamed hysterically, "*Martak! Martak!*"

Chapter Twenty-Two

THE GOLDEN IRIDESCENT GLOBE

Aboard the ship, Martak held the failing Rosy as time ticked away. Releasing her from Evil's grasp was all that mattered. He had to break the hold of the malevolent tune that compelled her to spin uncontrollably until she collapsed. *But how?* he wondered desperately. *What had she learned about the evil source that beckoned the destruction of her innocent soul?* He vowed that nothing would stop him until he had pried loose her secrets.

His initial coaxing had led Rosy to reveal what she knew about the strange force twirling her life away, but the full answer still eluded him. Holding her now in his arms, she cried out in despair. "The voice, the voice," she repeated. "It's so beautiful. If only I could find it." These were the last words he heard before exhaustion claimed her consciousness.

Martak was aware that little time remained before the ship's bell would ring twelve times and the Princess turned eight. Could she survive until then? At this point, it seemed impossible. She lay limply in his arms, enslaved and entranced by Evil.

Martak's thoughts turned inward, seeking his own best instincts for guidance. He recalled a lesson imparted long ago by his Guide—in hunting, the most subtle but dangerous device is deceptive appearance, for it is the least obvious snare that catches the wiliest of game.

Am I missing a snare? Martak wondered. *Is that what you are pointing me toward, my Guide?*

Martak's mind raced feverishly over the facts he knew. *Rosy spins for hours to the sound of a mesmerizing tune and a voice that only she can hear. I can't stop her, and she gets weaker and weaker as the melody becomes a whir and she spins faster and faster.*

Spins. Hours. Sick. Hmm...Any child who whirled for hours would probably be just as sick as Rosy. Could it be that spinning is not the real danger but only camouflaging the snare? What is Evil's game? What am I missing?

Little sand remained in the hourglass when Rosy stirred once more. Opening her eyes, she looked up at Martak and whispered, "Please put me down. I feel better now," as she began to wriggle free from his grasp. Afraid to let go of her so close to midnight, yet knowing how much she had been through, Martak cautiously placed her on the deck.

Smiling weakly, Rosy leaned over and gave Martak a peck on his cheek in thanks. For an instant, Martak let himself relax in the warming glow of her tender gesture. That was all Rosy needed. She flew from him as a trapped cat would from a distracted hound, running to the ladder that led to the ship's hold.

Sliding—not even stepping—down each deck's ladder and tipping the last one at the bottom to delay Martak from pursuing her, Rosy fled, possessed by Evil's influence, into the deepest part of the ship. Searching wildly for the tune, she found her way to the ship's armory. A startled Martak reacted swiftly, but not fast enough to prevent Rosy's descent. As he peered down at the fleeing child, he knew that unless he reached her quickly, he could not protect her and her fate would be sealed.

"I am here, over here. Come to me, child. Come to me," were the words Rosy heard as her eyes searched hungrily for the source of the seductive voice.

"Where are you?" she called out, unable to hear Martak's cries for her to stop. "Where are you?" she repeated until, gasping in awe, she exclaimed, "Ah, there you are!" Rosy stood transfixed by beauty as magnificent as her innocent soul. At last, she had found the source of the voice, and it was more glorious than she could have imagined—a glowing, golden, iridescent globe she could just reach out and touch.

Martak did not hesitate. As a nesting mountain eagle launches itself upon the winds to battle for the safety of its young, Martak flung himself into the hold, his hands grasping the fabric of his garment as his arms stretched out like wings to catch the air below.

It was just before midnight. Rosy's small, tender hand reached out eagerly toward the orb that would determine her destiny and the future of the Kingdom—just as Martak soared into the hold like an avenging raptor and raced to the ship's armory.

At the very instant he saw Rosy with her hand outstretched, both he and the Princess heard Marianna screaming for her beloved.

"*Martak! Martak!*"

Chapter Twenty-Three

THE CLIMAX

The air was filled with Marianna's painful cries. Then, as if by the hand of an ever-watchful Good, the ship bolted in the water. The sudden jolt thrust the golden globe out of Rosy's reach just as Martak tackled her, tumbling both of them to the floor. Struggling to control the flailing Princess, who fought madly to embrace the mesmerizing object, Martak lifted her to her feet and came face to face with the golden orb.

Alas, he too was threatened by its power, as he shared a hidden bond with Rosy.

Years ago, Martak's parents had been led to a pool near the forest where, reflected in the clear water, they saw the youthful image of their handsome, spirited, ten-year-old son thriving in his woodland home under the influence of his Guide, Good's most trusted hand. With a keen mind, natural ability and unspoiled grace, Martak continued to grow to manhood as he mastered the ways of the wild, never suspecting he was being groomed for a greater destiny.

Grasping a sword from the nearby armaments, Martak swung at the evil globe with all the power of his enraged soul.

On that fall evening so long ago, Martak's parents were overcome with heartfelt longing for him. While he had been beyond their reach for so many years, he remained at the center of their hearts. Each day was filled with sadness and despair knowing that he would never experience the depth of their love nor understand how much they missed him.

It was then they accepted that the only way to bring him back into their lives was to drive Evil away. With the safety of the Kingdom and their son's future at stake, they prayed they might have a second child. For as Good had provided, if a second child reached its eighth birthday without either child embracing the globe, Good would prevail and Evil would be banished. The threat to the Kingdom and to their son would be gone and he could come home.

A year later, a girl was born to this seemingly childless couple. But, before the birthing process ended, a second baby—a boy—unexpectedly pushed from Martak's mother's womb.

At the very same time, in another part of the Kingdom, the Queen was writhing in mirrored agony, tossing and turning, screaming with every contraction, trapped in a circle of pain. Beaded sweat coated her body and she clenched her teeth in delirium, pleading for a potion to banish the waves of anguish—even as she prayed she would soon give life to the heir to the throne. Her suffering wore on through the night, and dawn brought only soul-wrenching grief and tears of despair. The Queen's child was stillborn.

Witnessing the joy of one mother and the agony of the other, Good was deeply moved. Two couples from two very different stations in life had just shared the rawest of all human experiences. But for the longest of times, they had shared far more, as each held an unwavering, unquestioning faith in Good and the power of that trust was not lost on her. Unwilling to stand by idly and watch the newborn daughter grow up unprotected from Evil's minions, Good intervened. For the second time, she appeared before Martak's parents, congratulating them on the birth of their two beautiful, healthy twins and blessing them. She then shared the story of the Queen and her grief.

Martak's mother was a simple, pious woman with a compassionate heart, who had also lost a child, albeit figuratively, and she felt the Queen's pain. She also feared the curse that would shadow her precious daughter until her eighth birthday. So, she listened intently as Good offered a plan to bring solace to the Queen while also safeguarding Martak's newborn sister.

Good proposed to entrust the baby girl to the royal couple to raise as their own. If done quickly, Evil might never know what had transpired and, blessedly, their newborn son, the third child, would remain with them and be safe from Evil's curse. The thought of raising one son while knowing their other children were under the protection of Good provided a measure of comfort. Martak's parents kissed their precious daughter good-bye and, with a wave of Good's hand, the baby girl immediately appeared in the crib at the palace nursery. Only the King, Queen and trusted midwife knew the secret of the Princess's birth. Daylight brought the announcement of an heir, and there was much rejoicing throughout the Kingdom.

Now, almost eight years later, those same children, so long shielded, stood unguarded in the thick of Good and Evil's climactic battle for absolute power. The outcome was in the hands of one person—Martak, Master of the Forest, disciple of Good's bravest warrior, first-born son of Good's chosen couple, brother of the Princess and her twin, Tanner.

On the main deck, the faint sound of the first mate striking the ship's bell to signal the countdown to midnight had already begun.

Martak stood frozen before the golden, iridescent globe as he heard Marianna call out his name across the lunar bridge that bound their souls. Her very spirit, so much a part of him, brought instant joy and summoned the image of her beautiful face and honey-colored hair reflected in the ever-more-enticing globe. He could not help but reach out to embrace her likeness. Evil danced with devilish delight, while Good prayed for restraint.

As Martak's hand nearly touched the globe, his mind's eye caught a vision of the captive Marianna. He saw her pain and suffering. Wild rage and fury welled up inside him. All tender thoughts vanished, replaced by a desire for vengeance as he felt her torment and humiliation. The beauty of the golden, iridescent globe disappeared, and in its place Martak beheld, for the first time, the true form of Evil's creation—a wretched, tarnished sphere.

Grasping a sword from the nearby armaments, he swung at the evil globe with all of the power of his enraged soul. Over and over he drove the blade with unrelenting anger. The sword sang in the hold's heavy air as Martak slashed the orb, and with each stroke it grew smaller and smaller until Evil vanished in a trail of smoke.

Evil was defeated. Good had triumphed. Candles on board the ship and throughout the Kingdom grew brighter and more intense, casting a warm glow in the night and gleaming with the promise of a new day.

His fury spent, Martak collapsed beside a motionless Rosy. In that moment of complete surrender to his body's limits, his thoughts returned to Marianna and how she had saved him and all that was good from Evil's dominion. Had it not been for her tortuous situation, he never could have resisted touching the tempting, glowing object. Had fate ordained Marianna to suffer at the hands of one evil, so a greater Evil would be defeated? It was a chilling thought, but both had done what destiny called for them to do.

All Martak knew or cared about now was rescuing his beloved.

Chapter Twenty-Four

THE RESCUE

Martak let out a shrill whistle, summoning a flock of golden eagles. Guided by moonlight, the fierce birds carried their master swiftly across the sea toward his beloved. But was there still time to save Marianna?

Marianna's screams had raised a fury and fire in two men—one who lived to protect her and the other whose every instinct was to violate her.

Hearing another man's name on Marianna's lips banished all pretenses from her tormentor's fevered passion. His loins now controlled his hands as they ripped at her robe and his lusting eyes beheld her naked body.

But that was his last pleasure, for even as he sought to thrust himself inside her, the Black Knight was about to share Evil's fate.

Glass shattered as Martak, riding a phalanx of golden eagles screeching their master's voice, broke through the bedchamber window. Loins bared for gratification found deadly revenge instead.

Torn from his intended prey by Martak's powerful grip, the Black Knight fought like a cornered wild boar. But he was no match for the rage that sprang from the young lover's soul. Martak pulled his hunting dagger from its sheath and plunged the blade deep into the Knight's chest, sending the predator reeling backward toward eagles awaiting their chance for blood. With ruthless abandon, the winged hunters sank their talons into the Knight and swept his body up and away—a direction his soul would never travel.

Martak rushed to Marianna's side. Bound to the bed throughout all that had transpired, she was beyond hysterical. Frightened, sobbing, and shivering from much more than just her nakedness, she thought she would go mad.

Martak quickly released the ropes that cut so deeply into her delicate skin and wrapped her in his cloak. Cradling her, he gently brushed her hair with his lips and kissed her forehead. He wiped away the uncontrollable tears pouring down her face, tears of humiliation mixed with tears of relief as he tenderly rocked her, trying to absorb her pain and whispering over and over, "You're safe now, my love, and so is the Princess." They were the only two things she wanted to hear, and she managed a grateful nod.

Martak swept up Marianna and carried her onto a balcony, where the fresh night air had a cleansing effect. She rested there in his arms, looking up at him with eyes that touched his soul, as he held her tightly, patiently and lovingly until her body stopped shaking. From the height of the balcony, Martak and Marianna watched as the Black Knight's guards lowered the drawbridge to escape, only to be crushed by the surge of wild animals rushing onto the castle grounds and unleashing their pent-up fury. The creatures stormed the sinister fortress, showing no mercy to man, beast or object as they ravaged the courtyard and interior rooms, slaughtering, their gleaming claws destroying every piece of furniture and overturning every twisted candle. Violent flames burst in all directions.

Martak guided Marianna safely through the carnage and they left the destruction behind them, heading toward a secluded valley in the nearby forest. Reaching the protected area, they were met by smaller forest creatures that scurried to make a bed of gentle grasses for their master and his mate.

From their refuge, Martak shared with Marianna all that had happened on the ship, and she told him about Tanner and her abduction. Together, the lovers watched the blazing fire paint the distant night sky red. Smoke billowed from the Black Knight's castle and by the wee hours of the morning, ashes were all that remained of the evil fortress.

Turning away from the inferno, the lovers lay entwined in one another's arms. First, Marianna heard it. A new sound. Soft humming. A gentle flutter. Then she saw it. A vision. Thousands of tiny butterflies gliding overhead. And then she felt it. A slight touch comforting her with warmth as swarms of butterflies summoned by Martak nestled together overhead and alighted on them, forming a soft blanket. Safe and together, Martak and Marianna drifted off to sleep beneath the stars.

The moon's light shone brightly on the lovers as their dreams merged, foretelling the same future—a life together that was just beginning...

A perfect whole.

Chapter Twenty-Five

Reunion

Distanced from the events that occurred long before their births but joined by destiny, Martak and Marianna lay peacefully together, their souls sharing a common dream. As with one heart and one mind, each lover focused on the other. In her sleep, Marianna felt the magnitude of his victory, while in his slumber, Martak sensed the peacefulness of her rest in his protective embrace.

But Martak did not sleep long. He awakened before dawn and, without disturbing Marianna, rose to gaze at the moon nestled among the stars. A solitary figure, surrounded only by the endless sky, he thanked the Heavens that his mission had been successful. Good had prevailed. Innocence was protected. Evil was banished. The shadows of the past were gone forever.

Yet the enormity of his accomplishment paled in comparison to the depth of his feelings for his beloved, and he lost himself in a montage of colliding thoughts and images. Her angelic face and her torment. Her musical voice and her painful cries. Her intelligence and her humiliation. Her steadfast love that gave him the strength to conquer and her suffering that drove him to kill.

While Martak was lost in thought, the sun began its ascent and the star-studded sky faded, but not before it had charted a steady course for the black and gold ship's safe return, under the watchful eye of the first mate. As the vessel sailed swiftly toward the Kingdom, Marianna awakened from her sleep, healed from the terrors of her captivity. The beautiful butterflies that had warmed and comforted her during the night now melded together into the most magnificent, shimmering gown. She looked as radiant as a fiery opal.

Good had dispatched one of her winged horses to the King and Queen with a message proclaiming Martak's triumph over Evil and the Princess's safe return in the morning on board the royal ship. Palace couriers quickly spread the word throughout the Kingdom, so all could be present at the harbor and rejoice in the good news.

The animals that had patiently stood guard over Martak and Marianna during the night now parted reverently, opening a pathway for the lovers as they proceeded together to the waterfront to meet the black and gold ship. A great lion bowed in deference, allowing Marianna to slip onto his broad back, while a pair of white doves joined wings to form a crown and nestled into her hair. The forest creatures followed their master and his mate to the nearby harbor as golden eagles circled overhead, their cries heralding the procession.

The sun was shining brightly when the mighty ship arrived. It was greeted by a beaming and grateful royal couple surrounded by merry villagers.

Rosy, accompanied by Good, was disembarking when Marianna caught sight of her. Marianna ran to the dock, her feet barely touching the ground, and knelt to catch the precious Princess racing into her arms. She hugged and kissed the child, never wanting to let go of the brave little girl whose fate had been perilously entwined with the Kingdom's future. Tears of happiness streamed down both their faces as Rosy clung with relief to Marianna, feeling safe and secure in her teacher's protective arms.

Eyes glistening and still trembling with emotion, Marianna slowly looked up, meeting Martak's steadfast gaze as he approached with the King and Queen. Excited to see her parents, the Princess unwrapped herself from Marianna's grasp and joyfully bounded to embrace the royal couple.

Marianna stood up, smiling at Rosy's reunion with the King and Queen. Turning to Martak, now by her side, she searched his face with heartfelt emotion. Looking into each other's eyes, they found in their depths all the love they shared and all the pain they had endured. He reached out his hands and she grasped his ten fingers as he pulled her into his protective arms.

Holding her closely, Martak tenderly kissed Marianna's face from the slope of her forehead to the curve of her neck and back again. Kisses initially meant to comfort turned to kisses that bespoke the burning desire he felt for her. As his lips brushed her cheek once again, she turned her head to meet them with the fullness of her own. Time stood still as their passionate embrace seemed to last for eternity. In that moment of pure joy, two half-souls united, never to be separated again. The earth rocked, while shooting stars exploded, lighting the sky with heavenly brilliance.

Victorious, the Master of the Forest, the Maiden, and the Princess walked hand in hand toward the Kingdom and the epic celebration that awaited them.

Epilogue

Her gifted radiance. His strong gentleness.
Each body unshared in love, they count only on themselves,
One to ten, no more, no less.
Then, as if by chance—but not—each stands
Before the other and desires
My toes ten, they touch yours,
My fingers ten, they touch yours, too,
And then they do,
His gentle pressure overtakes the edges of her being.
Her radiance embraces all that can be sensed
Until both come as one to find the magic of the touch,
The sound, the sight, the scent, the taste of the other's to be their own.
Two hearts on fire with love join fevered minds of two
In a converging dance of one.
Souls, once half, unite and pour into seamless skin
Protecting this true love from all it will ever confront,

A perfect whole.

The End

Photo by Herbert Ascherman, Jr.

About the Author

Ten Fingers Touching is the first work of fiction and a true labor of love for Ellen A. Roth.

The genesis of *Ten Fingers Touching* has rested within Ellen for some time. As a young child, she was enthralled with fairy tales and spent countless hours reading and dreaming.

She devoted the early years of her professional career to the arts, studying museum curatorship and obtaining an MFA from Syracuse University. After moving to Pittsburgh, Pennsylvania in 1974, she became a registered art therapist and worked with emotionally disturbed and developmentally disabled children, while also earning her Ph.D. from the University of Pittsburgh's School of Education. Her experience as a mental health professional showed her how the power of imagination unlocks emotions in individuals of all ages.

In 1991, Ellen co-founded Getting to the Point, Inc., a premier relocation consulting firm that specializes in helping corporations attract highly sought executive talent to Pittsburgh by better understanding and addressing the needs of the trailing spouse. She combines her business savvy and communication skills to show individuals and families the quality of life that Pittsburgh offers.

Ellen has published numerous professional papers and articles. She is actively engaged in community service and is a member of the National Speakers Association.

Ellen was named one of the Best 50 Women in Business in Pennsylvania and honored as a Woman of Distinction by Girl Scouts Western Pennsylvania, and is a recipient of the YWCA Tribute to Women Leadership Award in the category of Entrepreneur.

Ellen shares her life with her husband, Dr. Loren Roth. She is immensely proud of her children and grateful to family and friends for their encouragement and support.

About the Illustrator

With an eclectic portfolio that runs the gamut from industrial design to children's books, John's career in advertising and publishing reflects his wide range of expertise in the multi-faceted world of illustration and design.

After years of perfecting his techniques with traditional media, John chose to apply his creative knowledge and artistic insight to the discipline of digital illustration. This seamless transition from canvas to computer has yielded some of the most imaginative and thought-provoking imagery in his career.

John lives and works as a freelance illustrator in Pittsburgh, Pennsylvania. His images grace the covers of books published by The Penguin Group, Tor Books, Harcourt Publishing, Llewellyn Worldwide and a myriad of other publications and periodicals for clients ranging from Japan to the UK.